The Little Vampire

Angela Sommer-Bodenburg

Illustrated by Amelie Glienke
Translated by Sarah Gibson

ANDERSEN PRESS

This edition first published in 2017 by
Andersen Press Limited
20 Vauxhall Bridge Road
London SW1V 2SA
www.andersenpress.co.uk

First published in Great Britain in 1982
Originally published in German as Der Kleine Vampir
by Rowolht Taschenbuch Verlag, Germany in 1979

2 4 6 8 10 9 7 5 3 1

British Library Cataloguing in Publication Data available.

ISBN 978 1 78344 576 9

Printed and bound in Great Britain by Clays Limited,
Bungay, Suffolk, NR35 1ED

CONTENTS

This book is for Burghardt Bodenburg, whose teeth are so brittle he could never turn into a vampire, and for Ada-Verena Gass, who can make a truly magnificent vampire face, as well as for Katja, who can shout: 'Eeeek! A vampire!' so beautifully – and for everyone who likes stories about vampires as much as I do.

Angela Sommer-Bodenburg

CHAPTER ONE
The Thing at the Window

It was a Saturday evening, the night when Tony's parents always went out.

'Where are you off to tonight, then?' Tony wanted to know that afternoon. His mother was in the bathroom, busy with her hair-curlers.

'Oh,' she said, 'I expect we'll have something to eat, and then perhaps go dancing.'

'What do you mean, perhaps?' asked Tony.

'Well, we haven't decided yet,' explained his mother. 'Is it that important for you to know?'

'No-o,' mumbled Tony. He thought it better not to tell her that he wanted to watch the thriller on television, which started at eleven o'clock. But it was too late: her suspicions were already aroused.

'Tony,' she said sternly, and turned round so she could look him straight in the eye. 'I hope you are not planning to watch something on television?'

'Oh, Mum,' protested Tony, 'what on earth gives you that idea?' Luckily, his mother had turned back to her curlers and so she did not see how red his face had gone.

'We might even go to the cinema,' was all she said. 'In any case, we shan't be home before midnight.'

So now it was evening, and Tony was alone in the flat. He lay in bed in his pyjamas, with the sheet drawn up to his chin, reading *The Truth About Frankenstein*. The story was about a travelling show. A man in a flowing black cloak had just come on the stage to announce the appearance of the monster. Suddenly, the alarm clock went off. Tony looked up from his book, frowning at the interruption. Crikey, eleven o'clock already! He just had time to switch on the television.

Tony jumped out of bed and pressed the switch. Then he snuggled back beneath the covers and watched as the picture slowly took form on the screen. It was still only the Sports Programme. His room was shadowy and dim; King Kong glowered down from the poster on the wall, his sneer exactly suiting Tony's mood. He felt wild and adventurous, as though he were the only survivor of a shipwreck, stranded on a South Sea island surrounded by sharks. His bed was his hide-out, soft and warm, and whenever he wanted to, he could creep in there and be hidden from sight. A heap of provisions lay at the entrance of this den, in fact the only thing missing was a keg of rum. Tony thought longingly of the bottle of apple juice in the fridge; the trouble was, in order to get it, he would have to cross the darkened hallway. Should he swim back to the ship? Braving the blood-hungry sharks which were lying in wait for their prey? Tony shivered. But the fact remained that castaways more often died of thirst than of hunger!

So, bravely, he set off. He hated the hallway; the light was permanently broken, and no one bothered to mend it. He hated the coats dangling in the wardrobe, looking like corpses. And then there was the hare! He thought with horror of the stuffed animal in his mother's workroom, even though he had enjoyed frightening other children with the thought of it. At last, he made it to the kitchen. He took the bottle of apple juice out of the fridge and sliced off a large chunk of cheese while he was about it. All the time, he had half an ear cocked to the other room to make sure the thriller had not begun. He heard a woman's voice announcing the start of the film. Tony tucked the bottle under one arm and hurried back.

However, he had not gone far, just into the hallway, when he noticed that something was not quite right. He stood still and listened...and suddenly it dawned on him what was wrong: there was silence from the television! That could mean only one thing: someone must have slipped into his room and turned it off! Tony could feel his heart miss a beat and then thud as if it had gone mad, and a strange lump seemed to move from his tummy to his throat and stick there. Terrible pictures appeared before his eyes, pictures of men with stocking masks, knives and guns, who broke into empty flats at night to steal, and who would allow no one to stand in their way. Tony remembered that the window had been left open, and a burglar could easily have climbed in over the next door balcony. All of a sudden, there was a crash! The apple juice bottle had slipped from under Tony's arm and had rolled across the hallway, coming to rest by the bedroom door. Tony held his breath and waited...but nothing happened. Perhaps he was just imagining all this nonsense about burglars? But if that is the case, why had the television stopped?

He picked up the bottle, and inched open his bedroom door. The first thing he noticed was an extraordinary smell, musty and mouldering like something in the cellar, but like burning as well. Was it coming from the television set? Tony quickly pulled the plug out from the wall. Perhaps the flex was smouldering.

Then Tony heard a strange rattling, which seemed to come from the window. He thought he could make out a shadow behind the curtain, outlined against the bright moonlight. Very slowly, with knees knocking, he forced himself nearer. The strange smell grew stronger, as if someone had been burning a whole box of matches. The rattling was getting louder too. Suddenly Tony stood rooted to the spot. On the windowsill, in front of the blinds which were moving gently in the night breeze, a Thing was sitting watching him. Tony thought he would faint with horror. Two small, bloodshot eyes gleamed at him from a deathly pale face framed by tangled hair, which hung in tendrils down to a grubby, black cloak. The figure opened and closed its gaping mouth, grinding its teeth in a most terrifying manner, and Tony noticed that these teeth were extremely white, and pointed like daggers. Tony's hair stood on end, and his heart practically stopped beating! The Thing at the window was worse than King Kong, worse than Frankenstein's monster, worse than Dracula even! It was the most hair-raising apparition Tony had ever seen!

The Thing seemed to enjoy seeing Tony frightened out of his wits, because it drew its enormous mouth back into a dreadful grin to reveal its needle-sharp, widely spaced teeth more clearly.

'A vampire!' gulped Tony.

And the Thing answered in a voice that seemed to come from the bowels of the earth: 'But of course I'm a vampire!' It sprang into the room and stood firmly in front of the door. 'Are you afraid?' it asked.

Tony could not make a sound.

'You're a bit skinny – not much flesh on you, I'll bet.' The vampire looked him up and down. 'Where are your parents?'

'I-in the cinema,' stammered Tony.

'Aha. Now let's see. Is your father a healthy fellow? Would his blood be...er, tasty?' The vampire giggled, and its teeth glistened in the moonlight. 'As I'm sure you are aware, we vampires live on blood!'

'I-I have very b-bad blood,' stuttered Tony hastily. 'I-I have to t-take pills for it.'

'Poor you,' said the vampire nastily, taking a step nearer.

'Don't touch me!' shrieked Tony, attempting to duck. All he managed to do was to knock the end of his bed, and a bag of jelly babies tumbled off onto the floor, the contents spilling out onto the carpet.

The vampire laughed with a rumble that sounded like a peal of thunder. 'Well, well! Jelly babies!' It looked almost human. 'I used to have these,' it mused. 'Grandma used to give them to me.'

It put a jelly baby into its mouth and chewed thoughtfully. Then all of a sudden it spat it out and began to choke and cough, swearing furiously as it did so. Tony took the opportunity of hiding behind his desk, but the vampire was so shaky after its coughing fit that it collapsed onto the bed, and for several minutes did not move. Then it pulled out a large, blood-spotted handkerchief from under its cloak, and blew its nose long and hard.

'That could only happen to me,' it grumbled. 'My mother did warn me.'

'Warned you about what?' inquired Tony curiously. He fell much more confident from his position behind the desk.

The vampire glanced furiously across at him. 'Vampires have very sensitive stomachs, stupid. Sweets are like poison for us.'

Tony felt quite sorry for him. 'Would you like some apple juice instead?' he asked.

The vampire gave a blood-curdling cry. 'What are you trying to do? Make me sick?' he yelled.

'I'm sorry,' said Tony. 'I was only trying to help.'

'That's all right.' Apparently, the vampire had not taken offence. In fact, thought Tony, it's a very nice vampire, in spite of its looks. Tony had always imagined vampires to be much worse.

'Are you old?' he asked.

'As old as the hills,' came the reply.

'But you're much smaller than me.'

'So? I was just a kid when I died.'

'Oh, I see.' Tony had not thought of that. 'And are you still...I mean, do you have a tomb?'

The vampire grinned. 'You could come and visit me if you like. But only after dark. We sleep during the daytime.'

'I know,' said Tony. At last, here was an opportunity to show off how much he knew about vampires. 'If vampires come into contact with sunlight, they die. So they have to hurry through their night's business in order to be back in tombs by sunrise.'

'What a clever fellow,' sneered the vampire maliciously.

'And if you discover the grave of a vampire,' continued Tony, warming to his account, 'you have to drive a wooden stake through its heart.'

It would have been better not to have said this, because the vampire uttered a chilling growl and sprang at Tony. But Tony was too quick. He shot out from under the desk and made for the door with the enraged vampire hard on his heels. Just before he reached the door, the vampire caught him. This is it, thought Tony. He's going to bite. But the vampire just stood panting in front of him, its eyes glowing like hot embers and gnashing its teeth – click-clack, click-clack. It took Tony by the shoulders and shook him. 'If you ever start on again about wooden stakes, it'll be curtains for you! Understand?'

'Y-yes,' stammered Tony. 'I-I really didn't mean to get at you.'

'Sit down!' barked the vampire. Tony obeyed. The vampire began to pace up and down the room. 'What am I going to do with you now?' it asked.

'We could listen to music,' suggested Tony.

'No!' shouted the vampire.

'Or play snakes and ladders?'

'No!'

'Or I could show you my postcard collection?'

'No, no, *no*!'

'Well, I don't know what we can do, then,' said Tony, giving up.

The vampire had paused in front of the poster of King Kong, and suddenly it gave a wild cry. 'Not that ape!' it yelled, and ripped the poster off the wall, and tore it into shreds.

'That's not very polite!' protested Tony. 'That was my favourite poster!'

'So what?' hissed the vampire. By now, it had discovered all the King Kong books on Tony's bookshelf, and page after page fluttered down onto Tony's bed.

'My books!' howled Tony. 'I bought them all with my pocket money!'

Suddenly the vampire paused, a happy smile on its lips. 'Dracula!' it breathed. 'My favourite book.' It looked at Tony with shining eyes. 'Can I borrow it?'

'Do. But promise to bring it back, OK?'

'Of course.' It stuck the book contentedly beneath its cloak. 'By the way, what's your name?'

'Tony. What's yours?'

'Rudolph.'

'Rudolph?' Tony had nearly burst out laughing, but luckily stopped himself in time. He did not want to get the vampire stirred up again! 'That's a very nice name,' he said. 'It suits you.'

The vampire seemed flattered. 'Tony's a nice name too,' he said.

'*I* don't think so,' said Tony. 'But my father's called Tony too, you see.'

'Oh.'

'And my grandfather before him. As if that made any difference to me.'

'Up till now, I had thought Rudolph was a pretty stupid name,' said the vampire, 'but you get used to it.'

'Uh-huh, you get used to it,' sighed Tony.

'Hey, are you often all by yourself like this at home?' the vampire inquired.

'Every Saturday.'

'Don't you get scared?'

'Sure. Sometimes.'

'Me too,' agreed the vampire. 'Especially in the dark. My father always says: "Rudolph, you're not a proper vampire. You're a coward!"'

They both laughed. 'Is your dad a vampire too?' asked Tony.

'Of course!' said the vampire. 'What did you think?'

'Your mum as well?'

'Yes. And my sister and my brother and my grandma and grandpa and my aunt and uncle...'

'My family is boring and normal,' said Tony sadly. 'My dad works at the office and my mum's a teacher. I haven't got any brothers or sisters. It's all very dull.'

The vampire looked at him sympathetically. 'There's always something happening with us.'

'Like what? Oh, do tell me!' At last here was a chance to hear a *real* vampire story!

'Well,' began the vampire, 'last winter, for instance. You remember how cold it was? When we woke up one day, the sun had already set. I was starving hungry, but when I tried to open the lid of my coffin, I couldn't! I drummed on it with my fists, I kicked at it with my feet – but it was no good. I could hear all the rest of the family doing the same thing, all around in the vault. And do you know what? For two nights we were iced in and couldn't get our coffins open. Finally it began to thaw, and we just managed it with the last of our strength.

We nearly died of starvation! But even that's nothing compared to what happened at the cemetery. Would you like to hear about that too?'

'You bet!'

'Well, it was on a...' began the vampire, but suddenly he broke off. 'Can you hear anything?' he whispered.

'Yes,' said Tony.

A car drew up and stopped. Its doors slammed.

'My parents!' cried Tony.

With a bound, the vampire was on the windowsill. 'My book?' called Tony. 'When...?'

But the vampire had already spread his cloak and was gliding away, a dark shadow before the pale crescent of the moon.

Quickly Tony drew the blinds and crept into bed. He heard the front door of the flat open and his father say: 'You see, Hilary? Everything's quiet.' Seconds later, he was fast asleep.

CHAPTER TWO
Parents Know Best

'What do you think about vampires?' asked Tony as he sat at the breakfast table and smeared honey on his toast. Although he looked as if he was only interested in his toast, in fact he was watching his parents' faces very carefully. First, they exchanged surprised glances, and then began to smile. They're not taking me seriously, thought Tony. They think I'm just being childish. If only they knew!

'Vampires?' asked his mother, hiding a smile. 'What on earth made you think of them?'

'Well,' said Tony, 'they used to exist in the olden days.'

'In the olden days,' mimicked his father, 'people used to believe in the weirdest things. Witches, for instance.'

'Witches!' retorted Tony scornfully.

'And dwarves, and ghosts and fairies...' added his mother.

'Haven't you forgotten Father Christmas?' said Tony furiously, and stirred his cocoa so violently that it slopped out of his mug and onto the table cloth. 'But I'll tell *you* something: vampires are a totally different kettle of fish!'

'Really?' asked his father sarcastically.

'Yes,' returned Tony. 'And anyone who thinks that vampires only exist in books –' ('Or at Hallowe'en

13

parties,' giggled his mother) – 'is either deaf and blind,' continued Tony in a slightly louder voice, then paused and finished on a soft, mysterious note, 'or very, very stupid.'

'Oh dear, you're making me quite nervous!' laughed his mother.

'It does seem strange that you and I have never seen one, dear, doesn't it?' smiled his father to her.

'Aha!' said Tony with satisfaction. 'That might happen sooner than you think!'

'Help!' said his mother, pretending to be scared.

'You'll see,' said Tony, and crammed the rest of his toast into his mouth.

'All I can see is that my cup is empty!' smiled his mother. 'Pour me out some more tea, would you, dear?'

Tony's father picked up the teapot, and as he poured, he winked at Mum.

Just let them laugh, thought Tony. He leaned back contentedly in his chair and thought of the coming Saturday.

CHAPTER THREE
The Give-away

The following Saturday began in the usual way. After breakfast, Dad went shopping. Mum had finished washing her hair, and was now busy looking for her hairdryer. Tony helped her find it.

'Are you going to a film again tonight?' he asked, trying not to sound too interested in the answer, as he plugged in the hairdryer behind the sofa.

'Possibly,' replied his mother. 'But there's a chance Dad might have to go to the office instead.' She took the hairdryer from him. 'Still, I might go to the cinema, even if he can't come.'

'Yes, why don't you?' encouraged Tony. His heart had sunk at the thought that his mother might stay at home that evening, because, of course, he was expecting a visitor! Meanwhile, his mother had switched on the hairdryer, and under cover of the noise, Tony made his escape to his room, where he had already made preparations for his guest. Any book which might have upset the vampire had disappeared from his bookshelf, like the last two King Kong books, the one about Tarzan, and the Superman stories. In their place were two new titles: one had a black cover with a picture of a giant-sized bat on it and in luminous red letters the words: *Twelve Chilling Vampire Tales*. The other had a purple jacket and was called *The Revenge of*

Dracula. Tony had deliberately put them where the vampire could not miss them. On the cupboard hung a picture which Tony himself had painted the evening before. It was a vampire rising from its tomb. Tony was proud of the deathly pale face with black, lidless eyes and a red, gaping mouth, from which protruded teeth as sharp as needles. His mother's reaction on seeing the picture had been encouraging. 'Ugh!' she had cried. 'Do you have to paint such revolting things?'

'What do you mean, revolting?' Tony had retorted, carefully touching up the teeth with white paint, so that they seemed to gleam even more brightly.

'Just look at its face! It'd give me nightmares!'

Tony merely thought it was bound to appeal to the vampire.

Now he studied his masterpiece with satisfaction. The hump of the graveyard in the background, with its tombstones and crosses, added the final gruesome touch. He wondered whether he should put in a couple of bats, but they were difficult to draw.

Instead, he settled himself on his bed to read. He had already started the first vampire story the day before. It was about a fancy dress ball, at which the guests appeared in every kind of costume. One had come as a vampire. His disguise was so good, that everyone had been afraid of him; and when midnight struck and everyone removed their masks, he stayed as he was . . . and suddenly everyone realised that he hadn't been wearing a mask at all!

While Tony was reading, his father came home, the telephone rang twice, the vacuum cleaner hummed, water ran in the bathroom; but none of this disturbed him. It was not until a piercing cry of pain broke out that he looked up from his story and listened. Had it come from their flat?

'My foot!' he heard his mother

'Why did you climb onto that rickety chair?' asked his father. That's why we have a stepladder.'

'Yes, yes,' grumbled his mother, 'but it's a bit late to think of that.'

'Try to stand up.'

'Ow!!'

'Can you turn it?'

'No!!'

'What's the matter. Mum?' called Tony.

'I've twisted my ankle!' replied his mother.

'Badly?' asked Tony.

'Yes. I'm going to sit with my foot up.'

Tony heard her hobble across the hall into the living room, and as he put the book back on the bookshelf, he wondered whether she would be able to get to the cinema that evening with a sprained ankle. He thought she might, as long as it was her right foot, because she only had to press the accelerator with that foot…However, to Tony's dismay, it was her left foot that was resting on the stool, and she was examining it gingerly.

'What a bit of bad luck,' she was saying. 'It's going to swell up.'

'You could put a cold compress on it,' suggested Tony.

'Good idea,' said Dad.

'Shall I quickly go to the chemist?' asked Tony.

'That would be kind of you, dear,' smiled his mother.

'Oh, it comes naturally!' said Tony cheekily.

'Oh yes?' growled his father. 'I can think of times when you . . .'

'Oh, stop bickering, you two,' interrupted Mum, and said to Tony, 'Be a dear and ask them what is the best thing for sprains.'

And so it happened that Tony spent the afternoon wrapping cold bandages soaked in vinegar round his mother's ankle. His father had long since gone off to the office, and Tony asked for the tenth time: 'There, now, doesn't that feel better?'

'I might begin to think you wanted me out of the house this evening,' remarked his mother.

'Oh? Why?' asked Tony, trying to sound hurt.

'Well, you needn't worry about Dad,' said his mother, smiling. 'He's safely in the office. But you hadn't counted on me having an accident and now you're doing your best to get me up and about again.'

'Oh Mum,' Tony said reproachfully, but he didn't sound very convincing.

'Anyway, whatever the reason, I've decided to stay at home tonight,' she went on. Tony felt himself go pale. 'And guess what? We'll have a lovely evening together, just the two of us.'

Tony could not reply.

'Hey, Tony! What's wrong?' asked his mother.

'N-nothing,' he stammered.

'We'll make some tea and play Ludo. It'll be such fun,' Mum continued, enthusiastically. 'Or we could watch television, if you'd rather. Is that why you're looking so worried? Did you think I wouldn't let you watch it?'

'No,' he said quietly.

'What's up, then?'

'Nothing,' he murmured, and looked out of the window. It was already getting dark. 'I think I'll go to my room. I feel like reading.'

Now *everything* was ruined! If only there was some way of warning the vampire! But how could he let him know? Tony threw himself down on the bed and buried his head in the pillow. He felt lost, helpless and bitterly disappointed. He had been looking forward to this night for a whole week! Suddenly, something knocked at the window – at first so softly that Tony thought he must have imagined it. But then it came again, and Tony sprang from his bed, ran to the window and tore the blinds aside: there on the windowsill sat the vampire! He smiled, and signalled to Tony to let him in. A quick glance over his shoulder reassured Tony that his bedroom door was shut, and with trembling hands and beating heart, he lifted the catch and opened the window.

'Hello,' said the vampire. 'It's good to see you.'

'Ssh!' whispered Tony. 'There's an enemy in camp!'

'Oh?' said the vampire.

'My mum,' whispered Tony. 'She's hurt her ankle.'

This did not seem to worry the vampire. Quite the contrary, he looked over to the door and licked his lips.

'You wouldn't d-dare...' stuttered Tony. The suspicion that had just entered his head was so awful that he did not dare say it out loud.

But the vampire understood very well. He looked rather embarrassed, and said, 'No, no, don't worry. In any case, I've just eaten.' He broke into a grating laugh, which made Tony wince. At that moment, the vampire noticed the books. '*Twelve Chilling Vampire Tales*,' he read, and sounding pleasantly surprised, he asked, 'New?'

Tony nodded. 'That one too – *The Revenge of Dracula*.'

'*Revenge of Dracula*?' Almost lovingly, the vampire picked up the book. 'That sounds fantastic.'

'Did you bring the other one back?'

'Ahem!' coughed the vampire, somewhat ashamed. 'My little sister has it at the moment. You'll get it back soon. She begged and begged, and I couldn't say no.' Putting *The Revenge of Dracula* quickly under his cloak, he said: 'You'll get both of them back next week.'

'OK,' said Tony. 'What do you think of my poster?' He pointed proudly to the picture on the cupboard.

'You did that?' The vampire smiled wryly. 'Not bad!'

'What do you think of the vampire?'

'Very good – except the mouth is a bit too red, perhaps.'

'Too red? But yours is just as red!'

'Yes,' said the vampire, and gave a little cough. 'But I have just – er – eaten!'

'Oh.' Tony felt rather put out. 'I hadn't realised that. Well, I can easily paint over it.'

Suddenly, he heard the living room door open.

'Mum!' he gasped. 'Quick! Into the cupboard!'

'Why?' asked the vampire, making for the window. 'I can go...'

'No! She'll only stay a moment,' said Tony. There was a knock on his bedroom door.

'Tony?' called his mother. 'Shall we have tea?'

'Er – um,' said Tony, trying hard to think of some excuse. 'I'm not hungry yet.' He opened the door a crack.

'What about a game of Ludo, then?'

I'd rather not. My book's got to a very exciting bit.'

'Hey, Tony!' said his mother anxiously, trying to past him into the room. 'Are you feeling OK? Is anything the matter?'

'No. Why?'

'There's such an odd smell in here. Tony, have you been playing with matches?' she asked sternly.

'Me? Certainly not.' Tony sounded hurt.

'There's something fishy going on here!' declared his mother, and, pushing Tony aside, she marched with determination into the room. She looked around suspiciously, but could not see anything obviously wrong. Then suddenly, her eye fell on the cupboard, and with a cry of, 'Aha! What's this, then?' she seized a mysterious piece of black cloth, which was sticking out from under the cupboard door.

'Ow!' came a muffled squeak from the cupboard. 'My cloak!'

Tony went white as a sheet. 'That's a friend of mine,' he said hurriedly, and moved protectively in front of the cupboard.

'*Why* is he in the cupboard?' asked his mother.

'Because ... he's afraid of the light!'

'Well, well, afraid of the light,' repeated his mother, unconvinced. 'I'd still like to meet him.'

'No. I'm sorry, that's impossible.'

'Why?'

'Because he's wearing his fancy dress outfit.'

'His fancy dress?' His mother sounded amused. 'Well, never mind. That's no reason for me not to meet him. Why don't you ask him to have tea with us?'

Tony shook his head. 'I'm sure he won't want to. He doesn't like tea.'

'No? Well, what does he like?'

A soft titter was just audible from the cupboard.

'Perhaps he'd like some squash?' suggested Tony's mother.

'Only if it's red squash!' cackled the voice from the cupboard.

Tony's mother was rather taken aback. 'We haven't got any red squash,' she said. 'Only soda water.'

'Urgh! Yucky soda water!' spat the vampire.

'OK. Nothing, then,' retorted Tony's mother, sounding offended. 'I'll go and make tea.' And with that, she stalked out of the room. She had hardly left, before the vampire opened the cupboard door and scrambled out. He looked even paler than usual and was rather short of breath.

'What are we going to do now?' asked Tony, pacing up and down with agitation.

'I must fly!' declared the vampire in sepulchral tones.

'You can't just leave me in the lurch! What'll I tell Mum when she asks where you've got to?'

'Oh, just say...' began the vampire, but at that moment, they heard Mum's approaching footsteps.

'Are you two coming?' she called.

Without further hesitation, the vampire sprang out of the window into the night and was gone.

'Where's your friend?' asked Tony's mother in surprise, as she came back into his room.

'He – ahem – well, he's gone to the fancy dress party.'

His mother looked at him doubtfully. 'Funny friends you've got,' she said.

'What do you mean, friends?' Tony rose to the attack. 'That's only one!'

'One – like that's enough!' smiled his mother. 'I hope I get to meet him properly next time. Anyhow, how did he get out of the flat?'

'Oh, he was very quiet about it,' said Tony. Crumbs, he thought, now she'll ask me how he got in without ringing the bell, and then what shall I say? But luckily, the ring of the timer in the kitchen diverted his mother's attention.

'Tea's ready,' she said. 'Are you coming?' Tony nodded. 'Good. Don't forget to close your window. Otherwise, moths will get into your room.'

'Or vampires!' added Tony, but his mother didn't hear. Sadly, Tony went over to the window. So that was Saturday over, the Saturday he'd been looking forward to so much. Oh well, perhaps next week would go better. He shut the window and pulled down the blinds.

While they were having tea, his mother asked: 'What was your friend's fancy dress costume like exactly?'

'Well, he was dressed as a – um –' Should he tell his mother? She'd never believe him. 'Well, he was going as a vampire.'

'A vampire?' echoed his mother. 'I wish I had seen him.'

'He'll probably wear it when he comes next time,' said Tony, comfortingly. Then, with a touch of daring, he added: 'He wears it nearly all the time.'

But his mother did not believe him. She merely laughed all the more, saying: 'Tony, you read too many horror stories. You'll be telling me next that he flew out of the window!'

'If only you knew,' said Tony crossly. Why is it that grown-ups always think they're so clever?

'Oh, Tony, don't let's quarrel about vampires!' said his mother, soothingly. 'Come on, what about that game of Ludo?'

'OK,' sighed Tony. He hadn't thought he *was* quarrelling about them! He set out the board and the counters and gave the dice to his mother. 'You start.'

'Why me?' asked his mother.

'Oh – got to give you a chance to win *something*!'

CHAPTER FOUR
A Second Cloak

'Well Tony, is that funny friend of yours coming tonight?' asked Tony's mother the following Saturday. She and Tony's father were going to the theatre this time, and had put on their smartest clothes: Mum had on a gold dress with a revealing neckline, and Dad was wearing a velvet suit and silk tie. Tony was ready to wave them off at the door. He coughed in slight embarrassment at the question, and answered, 'Ahem, well – maybe, if he's not already going to a fancy dress party.'

'What?' asked Dad. 'Who's going to a fancy dress party?'

'Tony's new friend,' answered Mum with a smile. 'He's always going to fancy dress parties.' Dad looked nonplussed. 'And guess what he goes as?' giggled Mum. 'A vampire!' At this, Dad looked so puzzled that Tony nearly burst out laughing, but he checked himself. There would only be an argument and then Dad might stay at home out of spite. You could never quite tell what grown-ups might do!

'Anyway,' said Mum, 'we'd like to meet this friend *one* day. And his parents too, of course.'

'His parents?' This was *too* much!

'Of course! We want to know what sort of family you are mixing with.'

'But I'm not mixing with his family,' protested Tony. 'Just him!'

'That's not the point. Where do they live, as a matter of fact?'

'Come on,' interrupted Dad. 'We must be off, Hilary.'

'Yes, yes, in a minute. Well, Tony?'

Tony had been hoping that he would not have to answer this one. 'Um, er, n-near the cemetery.'

'Where?' His mother was horrified, but Dad took her firmly by the arm and drew her downstairs.

'Don't let your imagination run too wild, son,' he said. 'Fancy dress parties all the time, vampires, cemeteries...whatever next?' He turned and waved.

'Bye dear.' His mother waved too, but looked a bit worried. Tony hoped her suspicions had not been aroused.

He shut the door and went back to his room. From his window, he watched his parents get into the car and drive away. He hoped Rudolph would soon be there. The sun had set and the moon was rising high and luminous in the night sky.

Six floors below him, at street level, the lamps were already lit up. A large black moth was fluttering down there, but it began to circle and climb steadily until it was level with Tony's window. A strange transformation began to take place: first, two feet appeared below the wings, then two hands and finally the familiar, spine-chilling face. It was the little vampire. He did a clever twist in mid-air, and came to land on the windowsill.

'God, you gave me a fright!' spluttered Tony.

'Don't say God!' The vampire shook himself.

'Do you always fly around in the shape of a moth?' asked Tony.

'I beg your pardon?' retorted the vampire. 'That wasn't a moth. That was a bat!'

'Oh,' said Tony, rather embarrassed. He always seemed to put his foot in it. But the vampire was not really cross. It is difficult for vampires to smile and look friendly, but Rudolph did his best.

'Are you by yourself?' he asked. Tony nodded. 'Good. I've brought something for you,' he added, and pulled out from under his own cloak a second one, just like his own. Tony had only to notice with a shudder the bloodstains and the smell of damp earth and mouldering wood which came from it, to realise that this was no fake!

'Try it on!' whispered the vampire.

'OK,' said Tony, doubtfully. He remembered the story of the fancy dress ball. Would *he* change into a vampire if he put this thing on? But in the stories he had read, the victim had to be bitten by a vampire as well for that to happen. But how did he know what this vampire had in mind? He shuddered suddenly, and backed towards the door, knees knocking.

'Hey, Tony!' The vampire sounded hurt. 'We're friends, remember?'

'Y-yes,' stammered Tony and in his confusion he tripped over his school satchel and sprawled full length on the floor.

The vampire helped him up. 'Do you really think I'd do anything to you?' he asked, looking at Tony steadily.

'N-no,' blushed Tony. 'It's just ... well, perhaps the cloak might ... but it's all nonsense!' he added bravely.

'Come on,' encouraged the vampire. He picked the cloak up off the floor and held it out to Tony. 'Put it on!'

For a moment. Tony thought he might be sick, but he gritted his teeth and pulled it over his head.

The vampire watched him with glowing eyes.

'Now you can fly!'

'Fly? Me?' asked Tony.

'Nothing easier!' laughed the vampire, and jumped onto Tony's desk, spreading his arms wide. 'Just imagine your arms are wings. Move them up and down, slowly and steadily. Up, down, up, down ...' He had hardly moved them once, before he was gliding round the room. 'See?' he said gleefully, landing on the bed. 'Now you do it!'

With unsteady legs. Tony clambered onto the desk and stretched out his arms.

'Now – fly!' ordered the vampire.

'I can't!'

'Yes! Just believe that you can!'

'*Can't!*'

'Can.'

'Oh, all right!' Suddenly, Tony didn't care if he fell on his head on the floor – he'd show the vampire who was right! Humans just *can't* fly! So he flapped his arms and jumped and – flew! The air *was* supporting him! It was like swimming under water – only much, much better!

'I *can* fly!' he crowed.

'Of course,' growled the vampire. 'Now, come with me!' He was already sitting on the windowsill, and looked round at Tony impatiently. 'We've got a lot to do tonight!' He stood up, and took off into the night. Tony's fear suddenly seemed to melt away, and without a moment's hesitation, he followed him out of the window.

CHAPTER FIVE
Goings-on at the Graveyard

'Where are we going?' asked Tony, as they flew along.

'Home, to get the books,' replied Rudolph.

'And where – I mean, where exactly are they?'

The vampire grinned. 'In my coffin of course! Where else?'

'Oh!?' gulped Tony. 'So we're going to the cemetery?'

'Yep. Scared?'

'Me? NO!'

'Don't need to be,' reassured the vampire. 'My family will all be out and about.'

Tony gave a sigh of relief. The wall of the cemetery was already coming into view.

'Ssh!' hissed the vampire, and caught Tony's sleeve. 'We must go carefully.'

'Why?' asked Tony, but the vampire did not answer. He seemed to be listening for something. 'Is someone there?' asked Tony anxiously. He guessed they must be somewhere on the far side of the cemetery. Last summer, the wall around it had been painted white, but here the stones were grey and crumbling, and moss was growing over them in places. 'Is it one of your – relations?' he asked.

The vampire shook his head. 'The Nightwatch-man doing his rounds,' he hissed. 'Come on, let's land.'

They had hardly hidden themselves behind the wall when they heard a loud wheezing. 'That's him!' whispered Rudolph. He looked worried. 'He's looking for us, you know.'

'Us?' cried Tony. He was frightened too now.

'Ssh! Us vampires, of course.'

'Why?'

'Because he can't stand us. What do you think he carries round in his pocket? A hammer and a wooden stake!'

'How do you know?'

'How do I know?' The vampire grew paler. 'Because he drove a wooden stake through the heart of my poor old Uncle Theodore.'

'Ugh!' exclaimed Tony.

'And all because Uncle Theo wasn't very careful one night, and was sitting on his tombstone just after dusk playing patience. The Nightwatchman simply marked which grave it was, and the next day, when it was light...' He paused and listened again. All was quiet. 'And ever since,' he continued, 'he hasn't left us in peace.'

'Couldn't you just...?' suggested Tony, and he snapped his teeth to indicate what he had in mind.

'Not him! He chews garlic from dawn to dusk!'

'Yuck!' exclaimed Tony. 'Garlic!'

'I wish he was like the old Nightwatchman,' sighed Rudolph. '*He* didn't believe in us, and besides, he had a gammy leg. He never used to come into this part of the cemetery, so we practically forgot that there *was* a nightwatchman.' He looked up at the sky thoughtfully. 'Such a nice man!'

'But the new one does believe in vampires?' asked Tony.

'Unfortunately, yes,' answered the vampire. 'And that's not all: he's determined to be the first nightwatchman in Europe to have a vampire-free cemetery,' He looked so upset that Tony felt quite sorry for him.

'Can't you do anything about him?' he asked.

'Like what?'

'You could move somewhere else.'

'Where? Who wants to have eight vampires roosting with them?'

'Hmm,' said Tony, and thought about that. 'What if you split up? I mean, if one of you went to one cemetery, and one to...?'

But the vampire shook his head decisively. 'Out of the question. We vampires stick together!' He stood up and peered over the wall.

'Well?' asked Tony.

'He's gone,' said the vampire. 'Now I can show you my coffin.'

Tony felt rather uneasy when they clambered over the wall and suddenly found themselves in the middle of overturned gravestones, crumbling crosses and thickly growing weeds. There was a deathly hush and quiet, and the graveyard looked creepy in the moonlight. Tony could not see anything that looked like a grave in use. The vampire smiled.

'It's well hidden, isn't it? You're almost standing on the family vault, and yet you don't know where it is.'

'Vault?' Tony was taken aback. 'I thought you each had your own grave.'

'A precautionary measure,' answered the vampire. 'We put all the coffins together in one underground vault, and there is only one entrance, which is well hidden – except of course, there's an emergency exit.'

He looked carefully around. Then he picked up a flat stone, overgrown with moss, which lay almost entirely invisible under the shadow of a yew tree. A narrow shaft leading underground was revealed.

'The entrance,' whispered Rudolph. 'I'll go first, then you follow. But don't forget to put the stone back after you!'

Feet first, the vampire slid down the shaft and under the ground.

CHAPTER SIX
In the Vault

Tony hesitated for a moment. Should he really follow Rudolph into the vault? How could he be sure it would be all right? But on the other hand, the vampire had never tricked him before, and it was probably much more dangerous to be left alone out here in the cemetery at night! What if one of the other vampires came back? No way! It was quite definitely better to trust Rudolph, who knew all the dangers in the cemetery, and to climb in after him!

Tony put his legs into the opening and let himself down slowly. At first, it seemed rather exciting to be sliding down into the earth like this, but when it came to actually letting go with his hands, his nervousness once more got the better of him. What would happen if there were quite a drop beneath him? Would he ever get out of this hole again? Then he heard Rudolph's voice quite close to him saying, 'Come on. Tony! Jump!' and he let go with his hands.

He landed on a platform. Above him, just out of reach, he could see the hole he had just come in by. He stood on tiptoe and pushed the stone over the gap. At first he could see nothing in the darkness that enveloped him, and it took a while before his eyes could make out the steps leading down into the inner chamber of the vault. There was only a feeble glimmer of light, and everything smelt of dankness and decay.

'Are you there?' Tony called out anxiously.

'Yes, come on,' came the answer.

Cautiously, step by step, Tony made his way downwards, and found himself in an inner chamber. It was a low-ceilinged room, which was only half illuminated by the slender candle burning in a niche near the entrance. Except for the coffins around the walls, it was completely empty. The little vampire was standing on the foremost coffin, a beaming smile on his face.

'Welcome to the Sackville-Bagg vault,' he cried, and then added proudly, 'Well, what do you think of it?'

'I . . .' began Tony, and hesitated. How could he say that he thought it was one of the nastiest places he had ever been in, and he thought the stink might make him sick at any moment?

'Not bad, eh?' enthused Rudolph.

'Why is it called the Sackville-Bagg vault?' Tony changed the subject.

'Because it's the last resting place of the Sackville-Bagg family, of course!' explained Rudolph.

'Is your name Sackville-Bagg too?' asked Tony.

'Yes! Rudolph Sackville-Bagg, if I may introduce myself!'

He made a funny little bow, and Tony noticed how thin and wrinkly his neck was. 'And now,' continued Rudolph springing down from his perch, 'I'll show you round the coffins!'

He picked up the candle, took Tony by the arm and went with him right into the vault. The flickering light of the candle threw ghostly dancing shadows on the walls. Tony's mouth grew dry with suspense.

'Here you see my dear grandmother's coffin,' announced Rudolph, pausing in front of a large coffin which was decorated with many woodcarvings. 'Sabina the Sinister Sackville-Bagg.'

'Why was she sinister?' asked Tony.

'Well, she was just called that in the old days,' replied Rudolph. 'She was the first vampire in the family, and had to make a name for herself.'

Tony looked at the coffin and shuddered. Just think what lay in it during the daytime!

'And this one,' went on the vampire, standing by the next one, 'is William, my grandfather. Sabina of course bit him first, and so he quickly took after her and was a very enthusiastic help to her on her nightly forays. In those days, he was known as William the Wild.' He giggled, as an afterthought.

'Did he have to – er – make a name for himself too?' asked Tony.

'No, not exactly. But he was renowned for his appetite,' answered Rudolph.

Tony felt as though a cold hand were running down his spine. 'Whose is that?' he asked hurriedly, moving on to the third coffin.

'That's my father's,' replied Rudolph. 'Frederick the Frightful Sackville-Bagg, the eldest son of Sabina and William Sackville-Bagg. Next to him is my mother, Thelma the Thirsty. My father was already a vampire when he married her, although my mother never knew anything about it. It was only when he brought her home to the family castle that...' He did not finish, just grinned and smacked his lips. 'And that,' he continued, 'is my coffin. You can get in if you like.'

'No thanks,' murmured Tony, 'I'd rather not.'

'Why not?' cried the vampire, and opened up the lid. The inside was lined with black silk, which looked a bit worn out in places. At the head, there was a small, black cushion, on which, Tony noticed, lay his two books.

'Is that all?' he asked, somewhat disappointed.

'What did you expect?' asked the vampire.

'Oh, I don't know,' said Tony. 'I thought coffins were a bit more comfortable.'

'Comfortable?' The vampire sounded surprised. 'What do you mean?'

Tony realised he'd said something wrong again. 'Well, a bit more roomy,' he hedged.

'Roomy?' cried Rudolph with feeling, 'There's plenty of room. There'd even be room for you in here with me.' He got in and lay down, pushing the books to one side. 'See? Plenty of room for both of us!'

'Yes, I see now. But still, I don't think...'

'Stop thinking, then, and just get in here,' said the vampire impatiently.

'Ah – er,' said Tony, quickly going on to the next coffin. 'I've been longing to know who this sweet little one here belongs to.'

The vampire peered out of his coffin. 'My little sister,' he said. 'But come on in here.'

'And what about this one behind here?' continued Tony, regardless. *Nothing* was going to get him into a coffin at the same time as a vampire!

'That's my brother's. Gruesome Gregory Sackville-Bagg,' said Rudolph, grinding his teeth.

'What's your sister called?' asked Tony, trying hard to divert the vampire. But at that moment, he heard a soft knocking sound, which seemed to come out of one of the coffins. He stood stock still with fright. Were they not alone in the vault after all? Had Rudolph tricked him? But the vampire looked just as surprised and horrified as he did!

'Ssh!' he whispered, climbing nimbly out of his coffin. 'That bodes no good for us. You must hide!'

'Hide?' cried Tony. 'Where can I?'

The vampire pointed to the coffin, whose lid still stood open.

The knocking noise came a second time, but now it was louder and stronger, and they could recognise clearly from which coffin it was coming. 'Aunt Dorothy!' gulped Rudolph, sounding really frightened now. His face had paled even more than normal, and his teeth were chattering as though he had frostbite.

'Quick, you must get in my coffin!' he whispered.

'If Aunt Dorothy finds you here, you're for it!' Tony did not have the strength left to argue, and let himself be led to the coffin and helped in.

'And no grumbling!' warned the vampire sternly, before he shut the lid. Then Tony was alone. Darkness black as pitch enveloped him, and the smell nearly made him sick. He could hear Rudolph's voice outside in the vault: 'I'm just coming, Aunt Dorothy.' A coffin lid creaked open and then a deafening row broke loose.

'What manners!' shrieked a shrill, high voice. 'Leaving me here in my coffin to starve! Another ten minutes and I'd have died of hunger!'

'But Aunt Dorothy,' said Rudolph, trying to calm her. 'Why didn't you open the lid yourself?'

'Why?' she scolded. 'Because I am so weak and exhausted that I could only knock. A minute more, and I would have passed out with hunger!'

From the heavings and groanings that now followed. Tony guessed that Aunt Dorothy was getting out of her coffin. 'Oh, I'm so weak and feeble,' she moaned. 'If only there were something to eat!' But suddenly her voice altered to a low hiss. 'What's this?' she cried. 'I smell humans!'

Tony's heart nearly stopped beating. What if she found him in here!

'Oh, Auntie,' reassured Rudolph. 'You must be making a mistake!'

'I *never* make mistakes,' declared his aunt. 'But I suppose it could be coming from outside.'

'Perhaps it's a man taking his dog for a walk,' suggested the vampire helpfully. 'In any case, you should hurry up, before he gets away.'

'Yes, you're right!' Aunt Dorothy's blood was up! 'I must be off!'

Tony heard her gallop off up the steps and push the stone to one side. Then everything was quiet. He held his breath and waited. Had Rudolph gone with her? But then he heard soft footsteps coming back down the stairs, and straight away, the coffin lid was opened.

'Hello!' said the little vampire, grinning. Tony lifted his head cautiously and asked: 'Has she gone?'

'Yes. She's off after that man who's walking his dog!'

Tony sat perched on the edge of the coffin. He suddenly felt dead tired.

'Well, you don't look very appetising!' said the vampire cheerfully.

'I want to go home,' said Tony in a small voice.

'Home? But the night's only just begun!' The vampire sounded surprised. But Tony had made up his mind.

'Oh, OK, then,' grumbled his friend. 'We'll fly back together. But don't forget your books!'

Barely ten minutes later. Tony was back in his own bed. He looked across at the window, which he had taken care to shut behind him, and the night looked black and scary outside. Then he shut his eyes, and fell fast asleep.

CHAPTER SEVEN
Rude Awakening

When Tony woke up the next day, the smell of lunch was already creeping round the flat. Tony sniffed: macaroni cheese, browned and crisped in the oven. Yum!

He wondered why he had slept so long, but then remembered that it was very late when he had eventually gone to bed, and the events of the night before went spinning through his mind like a film. He wondered where the cloak was. He was sure he'd put it with his other clothes on the chair, but it wasn't there any more. Perhaps his parents had found it! The thought of that made Tony suddenly very wide awake. He could hear the sound of the washing machine, and his heart sank. He jumped out of bed, and ran into the kitchen, where his father was sitting at the table peeling apples.

'Morning, Tony,' he greeted him cheerfully.

'Morning,' mumbled Tony.

'Still tired?' grinned his father.

'No-o,' said Tony, and cast a sidelong glance at the washing machine. It was certainly washing *something*, but the lather made it impossible to recognise what!

'Are you looking for something?' asked his father.

'No, no,' said Tony nonchalantly. He went to the fridge and poured himself a glass of milk. 'What's in the washing machine?' he asked, taking a gulp of milk so that his father should not realise how concerned he was.

'Why do you want to know?'

'Because . . . I had some things that needed washing too,' he said with a rush. If only his father would turn off the machine for a moment, he could find out whether the cloak *was* inside, and if necessary, he could surreptitiously remove it!

'What needed washing exactly?' asked his father.

'Socks,' said Tony firmly. 'My white socks.'

'Well, well, your white socks,' echoed Dad, and it was obvious he was laughing about something. 'Well, I'm sorry, but they couldn't go in with that load. It's all the dark things at the moment.'

'All the dark things?' Tony could not help sounding anxious. 'Was there anything of mine in there as well?'

'Yes,' said his father unhelpfully.

'Oh.' Tony paused. 'What of mine?'

'You'd better ask Mum about that.'

'Where is she?'

'In the living room. She's doing the mending.'

'The mending?' Tony was really worried now. A new and equally perturbing thought had just occurred to him, as he remembered how many holes there were in the cloak. 'Is she mending . . . socks?' he asked hopefully.

'Far from it,' smiled his father. 'She found an enormous bit of black cloth, full of holes . . .'

'Holes?' cried Tony. 'Oh, no!' and he rushed off into the living room. He could not care less now if his father saw how worried he was.

His mother was sitting by the window, and was busy trying to pull a long thick piece of black wool through the eye of a rather narrow needle. And on her lap lay... Rudolph's cloak!

'Urgh!' she said, as Tony appeared. 'This really stinks!'

'It – it b-belongs to a friend of mine,' stuttered Tony.

'I know,' smiled his mother. 'The poor boy. It's such a tattered old thing. The holes are big enough to stick your fingers through!'

'I don't think he wants them sewn up,' said Tony.

'Why on earth do you think that?' asked his mother.

'Well, he said so,' said Tony.

In the meantime, his mother had finished darning the second hole, and was trying to thread the needle for the third. 'I don't believe it!' she said confidently. 'No one would want to go around in anything as full of holes as this! Perhaps he hasn't got anyone to sew them up for him. No, no,' she said, adamantly, 'I'm quite sure he'll be pleased to have it mended. What's his name, by the way?'

'Rudolph,' grumbled Tony. He had already reached the door. What he really felt like doing was to howl with rage: it was all a plot, and Dad had just been acting so innocent! Well, just wait! He'd show them!

'Do you want anything to eat?' called Dad from the kitchen.

'No,' said Tony.

'The macaroni cheese'll be ready in ten minutes!'

'OK,' said Tony. He went back to his room and lay down on the bed. What a mean trick to have played on him, to pinch his cloak and darn it, without even asking him first. And not only that – to have gone on darning it, even when he'd specifically asked her to stop! Tony was angry with himself too for having left it lying around, even though he knew that his parents always looked into his room in the morning to see if he was still asleep.

But perhaps it wasn't such a bad thing that his mother was mending the cloak. In fact, if it didn't have so many holes, the vampire would probably be able to fly better in it. Mum was right after all, and he ought to be thankful for it! At that moment, he heard his mother coming across the hall, so he quickly stood up and began to make his bed. He was just shaking out the pillows when she knocked on his door.

'Tony?'

'Yes. You can come in.'

'Here,' said Mum. 'One cloak, good as new!'

'Thanks,' muttered Tony. He took the cloak from her and put it on a chair.

'I'd have liked to have washed it,' went on his mother. 'But then it wouldn't have dried for a long time. And Rudolph wants it back soon, doesn't he?'

'Yes, he does!' said Tony quickly.

'Why don't you take it over to him today, then?'

'Today? Oh, well –' Tony was at a loss for words. 'He's – er, sleeping today.'

'What?' laughed his mother. 'Do you know how late it is?'

'Lunch is ready!' called Dad from the kitchen.

'He really is a funny friend, if he sleeps all day,' said Mum, giving Tony a searching look. 'You must tell us more about him during lunch.'

'Oh. Er, I'm not very hungry today,' said Tony, even though his tummy was churning in anticipation of the macaroni cheese.

'Nonsense!' said Mum, and Dad called, 'He hasn't even had breakfast yet!'

'Oh, all right,' grumbled Tony. In any case, macaroni cheese was his favourite lunch, although today he didn't really feel like it. He thought worriedly how it would be at the table, when every mouthful would be punctuated by questions as to why Rudolph slept so late.

'Good, isn't it?' said Dad, who was already on his second helping.

'Delicious!' agreed Mum. 'Tony doesn't seem to be enjoying it much, though.' Tony felt himself go red. 'Tell me,' said Mum suddenly. 'What's Rudolph's surname?'

Tony's heart stood still. 'Why?'

'Why? Because I'm interested, that's all!'

'Bagg,' muttered Tony.

'What?' Tony's mother could not believe it. 'Rudolph Bagg?'

'Sackville-Bagg, actually,' corrected Tony. 'Rudolph Sackville-Bagg.'

'That's even worse,' laughed Dad.

'Tony Peasbody isn't much better!' said Tony, heatedly.

'Now, now,' grinned Dad. 'We're all called Peasbody, you know!'

'Yes! But it's all right for you,' cried Tony. 'You're grown-ups! People don't laugh at you!'

'Just be thankful you're not called Peasbody-Bagg!' remarked Mum.

But Tony did not think that was particularly funny. Grumpily, he fixed his eyes on his plate. They were always laughing at him.

'Tony,' said his mother, 'where's your sense of humour?'

'Can I get down?' was all Tony could reply.

'In a moment,' said his mother. 'What are you going to do about the cloak? Will you take it over now?'

'Er – OK,' said Tony.

'I could drive you over there,' offered Dad.

'Over where?'

'To your friend's house, of course,' said Dad. 'I'll be going past the cemetery.'

'Th-the cemetery?' Tony had gone white as a sheet.

'I thought you said he lived near the cemetery?' said his mother.

'Y-yes, he does,' murmured Tony.

'Well, then, you can show me where exactly,' said Dad.

'And ask him over,' added Mum.

'B-but...' stuttered Tony helplessly. 'He'll still be asleep, and anyway, I feel like a walk...'

'Good heavens!' exploded his father. 'Tony Peasbody feels like a walk! This *is* a turn-up for the books!'

'Let him, then,' said his mother, and turning to Tony, she added: 'But if you go on your own, I insist you ask him over here. We want to meet him!' She paused for a moment. 'Ask him for Wednesday. Then I'll be able to make a cake for tea.'

'I-I'LL be off, then.' Tony backed away.

'Don't forget the cloak!' called Mum. 'And remember: Wednesday, at four o'clock!'

CHAPTER EIGHT
The Heart-shaped Gravestones

Sunday afternoon from lunchtime until four o'clock was the most boring time of the whole week, thought Tony – it always seemed to go so slowly! Up till one o'clock, everything smelt deliciously of the Sunday lunch, but that was quickly eaten up, and then everyone went to sleep. From then on, children must preferably not be seen, and certainly not be heard! Playing football in the street or zooming around on your bicycle was not worth the risk!

So when Tony took the lift down to the ground floor, it was not surprising to find it completely empty. The street was dead quiet too. Not a car passed. Tony wandered along, balancing on the kerb, and swinging the plastic bag with the cloak in it. He knew that his parents were standing on the balcony waving to him, but he stared stonily in front of him. They could wave till the cows came home for all he cared. It would teach them if he never came back alive! In fact, he was rather vague about what exactly he was going to do at the graveyard. How on earth was he going to get the cloak into the tomb in the daylight? And how on earth was he supposed to invite Rudolph to tea? Should he leave a note? Luckily, he had thought of this, and had brought a pad of paper and a pencil with him. But he was quite sure that there was no letter-box at the tomb! And if he were to go into the vault himself, and leave the note on Rudolph's coffin, the other vampires would be sure to wake up, and then what would happen? Tony walked more and more slowly the nearer he got to the cemetery. Finally, he came to a standstill. He knitted his brows and stood deep in thought.

'Hi, Tony!' came a voice.

'What are you doing here?' he asked and blinked. Before him stood Nigel, a boy from Year Six, whose nickname was 'Blabber-Mouth' because he was always gossiping.

'What brings *you* here is more to the point!' he said, standing with legs apart and arms folded, blocking Tony's path.

'I'm...' Tony tried to be vague. I'm just going for a walk around here.' That was a very stupid answer, he knew, and he realised it would not satisfy Nigel, but he had not been able to think of anything better in time. He wondered if he should have told him the truth, but Nigel would never have believed him. If he had, he might have disappeared without further persuasion!

'I'm just going for a walk around here!' mimicked Nigel with a sneer. 'Can't you think of a better reason than that?

'Yeah,' said Tony. 'I'm going to visit a friend of mine.'

'Anyone I know?' asked Nigel with menace in his voice.

'Doubt it,' grinned Tony cheekily, 'unless you know any vampires!'

Just for a moment, Nigel was too taken aback to reply, but then he said scornfully: 'Vampires! That's a good one! I'll think I'm at the flicks next!' He shook his head, and then towered menacingly over Tony. 'Just clear off, you! And don't let me catch you wandering around here again!'

'OK, OK,' said Tony. 'Don't lose your cool, man.' And he went on his way, swinging the bag and whistling. Nigel mustn't think that he had frightened him, even if he were two forms above him! He reached the wall of the cemetery without looking back. It was painted white and so high that Tony could only see the tops of the yew trees over it. Just before he reached the gates, he stopped, and looked furtively around, but Nigel had vanished. Tony waited for another minute or two, but when still nothing happened, he opened the gate and slid inside.

The silence of the cemetery stole over him, and he was aware of the smell of earth and flowers. Not so bad after all, thought Tony, and feeling less spooky, he walked on. If it had not been for the many crosses and gravestones, with crazy things like 'Rest in Peace' engraved on them, he might have thought he was walking through the park. The only odd thing was that he did not see anybody else, but perhaps Sunday afternoon was not the right time for visiting graveyards. Never mind, it was all the better for him – he could be sure of not being disturbed.

He went on down the main pathway. He had been here before with his mother, when she came to see that all was well with his relations' graves. So he already knew that the wilder part of the cemetery began behind the chapel, which lay ahead of him at the end of the path. He always thought this. chapel looked rather cosy; it was built like a normal house, except that it didn't have any windows, only an enormous door made of iron. And although the chapel itself looked old and weathered, at the door hung a brand new, and obviously frequently used padlock, which Tony found the strangest thing of all, because not once had he ever seen anyone go in or come out of the place.

Today, he crept past the building with an uneasy feeling in his tummy. Nothing had changed about it, even the padlock gleamed in the afternoon sun. He wondered whether the chapel was empty. And if it wasn't, what was lurking inside? Nothing pleasant, he decided, and was reminded of the story, *Night in the Morgue*, which he had read not long before: a man had spent a night in a morgue in order to win a bet, and at first had thought he was alone. But when the moonlight shone in through the window, one of the cabinets had begun to open, and out came... Tony felt a cold shudder run down his spine at the thought, even though the sun was shining!

Suddenly, he was in a hurry to drop the cloak and get out of the cemetery. Who knew what might be lurking there? Vampires weren't the only things Tony read about – in fact they were probably the most harmless...what about the bodies that weren't really dead? Tony had once read about a woman who knocked at the lid of her coffin in increasing despair, until finally she died of exhaustion.

Tony quickened his steps. If anyone were to start knocking, he, Tony, certainly would not go to investigate! The best thing would be to run so fast that he wouldn't even hear any knocking! He hadn't forgotten old Aunt Dorothy in the vault the night before.

By now, Tony had left the part of the cemetery where the paths were raked and the hedges neatly trimmed. Here, behind the chapel, the grass grew knee-high, and he had to make his way through brushwood and weeds. But he could see the wall of the cemetery in the distance. The yew tree must be round here somewhere, and with it, the entrance to the vault. As he went further, he suddenly thought he could hear steps on the gravel behind him. A cold shiver ran through him. Who or what could be following him? Something that had come out of the chapel?

But the next moment, all was quiet again, and he dared to look round – the cemetery lay still and quiet as before. He must have imagined the footsteps; after all, it was pretty lonely here, and it wasn't surprising you began to imagine things!

Tony nearly stumbled over a gravestone that lay hidden in the grass. It was an unusual stone, in the form of a heart. And across it in flourishing, barely legible letters was written: Frederick Sackville-Bagg, 1803–1850.' Tony shivered, for if these dates were right, Rudolph's father had already been dead for over a hundred years! A few paces further on, he discovered another stone, also in the shape of a heart, which bore the inscription: Thelma Sackville-Bagg, 1804–1849', and nearby he found the grandparents' stones: 'Sabina Sackville-Bagg, 1781–1847', and 'William Sackville-Bagg, 1780–1848'. A metre or two further on lay the gravestone of Great-Aunt Dorothy, and near that, Uncle Theodore. And each one was in the same heart-shape. Tony thought it was altogether too pretentious. What on earth was the heart supposed to mean, anyhow? Firstly, love – Tony giggled – and secondly, blood! Everyone knew that it was the heart which pumped blood through the body.

As Tony compared the dates, it occurred to him that the vampires had all died in a particular order, and all within a year of one another: first Sabina, then William, Thelma, Frederick, Dorothy and Theodore. Did that mean that each one had...? And what about the children? Who had...? Where were their gravestones anyway?

Tony looked and looked, but he could only find ordinary grey stones which certainly were not covering any vampire's grave. Perhaps the little vampire and his sister just didn't have any stones. They were probably the last of the Sackville-Baggs to die, and there was no one left to give them a proper vampire burial. As he was musing about this, he heard a rustling in the bushes near him, and turning round, he saw the grinning face of Nigel.

'You?' was the only thing he could think of to say.

'That's surprised you!' Nigel pushed his way out of the bush with a complacent grin on his face. 'Why do you look so scared? Did you think I was a ghost?'

'Er – I,' murmured Tony. 'I thought it was...'

'A gobbledy-gook!' smirked Nigel.

'No! I thought it was my friend,' explained Tony. 'We arranged to meet here, but he hasn't turned up yet.' He wondered if Nigel would believe him, but he couldn't think of any better explanation at the time.

'Oh yeah? Think I buy that?' said Nigel scornfully, and then, pinching hold of Tony's chin and forcing his eyes up to meet his own, he continued: 'You think I'm stupid or something?'

'Ow!' protested Tony, but Nigel pinched even harder.

'You watch it,' he said menacingly. 'Just tell me what's going on here.'

'Leave off first,' demanded Tony.

'OK,' agreed Nigel, and took a step backwards. 'So?'

'I wasn't lying,' said Tony. 'I really am meeting a friend here.'

'And what's this friend called?'

'Rudolph. Rudolph Sackville-Bagg.'

Nigel's expression became suspicious again. 'And what are you both up to in the graveyard?'

Tony's mind worked feverishly. On no account must he mention the vault, for Nigel would surely blab, and then the whole vampire clan would be lost.

'We-er, we were going to look for vampire graves!' he said finally.

'Vampire graves!' scoffed Nigel with a yawn. 'Kids' fairy tales!'

'No, no,' protested Tony. There were meant to be vampires in Rudolph's family way back!

'Ha, ha!' said Nigel loudly but not sounding the least bit amused.

'There's something special about their graves,' went on Tony.

That seemed to catch Nigel's attention. 'Something special?' he echoed.

'Yeah. The gravestones.' Tony let his voice sink to a whisper, and he looked furtively around him. They're in the shape of a heart!'

'A heart?' echoed Nigel.

'Don't you see?' explained Tony. 'Hearts mean blood!'

Nigel's lips curved in a scornful smile. 'What rubbish,' he said. 'You'd never find even half a gravestone in the shape of a heart!'

Tony had to make an effort not to laugh out loud. 'We'll see, we'll see,' he giggled. 'And anyway, it doesn't hurt to look.'

'So why weren't you looking?' asked Nigel unkindly.

'Because I was waiting for my friend,' said Tony patiently.

One thing was good, anyway: he had turned Nigel's interest to the gravestones. He could see that Nigel *was* intrigued, because he kept shifting from foot to foot.

'Shall we bet on it?' said Nigel at last. 'Three pounds for you if we find the gravestones, and five pounds for me if we don't.'

'Why do you get five and me only three?' asked Tony crossly.

Nigel put on his lofty, older-boy smile. 'Because three for you is the same as five for me.'

'That's not fair,' said Tony. 'I'd have to pay you five if I lost!'

'Are you going to lose, then?' mocked Nigel.

'Well,' said Tony, unable to conceal a smug smile, 'We'll see...'

'Right, then, let's get going!' said Nigel. 'I'll start here, and you go over there!'

Tony had only taken a few steps towards the chapel, when he heard Nigel cry out. 'Tony, come here, quick! I've found them!'

Tony tried to look surprised. 'Really?' he said.

Nigel was beside himself. 'God!' he said, again and again. 'Gravestones in the shape of hearts! Look at this one: Frederick Sackville-Bagg, 1803–1850, and Thelma Sackville-Bagg, 1804–1849.' He looked at

Tony with wide eyes. 'Hey! Didn't you say your friend was called Sackville-Bagg too?'

Tony tried not to look too pleased. 'Yep,' he said, with a shrug.

By now, Nigel had found the other gravestones, and his voice faltered as he listed the names. 'Sabina, William, and here – Dorothy. What weird names they all had!' The two boys smiled. 'But they've all been dead for years,' Nigel continued. 'Or do you think they still fly around?'

'I thought you didn't believe in such fairy tales?' teased Tony.

'Well, no, I don't,' mumbled Nigel. 'But this gravestone thing...' He paused, then said: 'Hey, didn't you say your friend was a vampire too?'

'Did I say that?'

'Sure. Back outside the cemetery.'

'Then perhaps I meant it,' said Tony.

Nigel took a step closer to Tony and looked at him warily. 'Did you mean it?'

Tony merely smiled. 'I could tell you many a tale if you believed in vampires.'

'Maybe I do believe in them now,' said Nigel. 'And if I don't, you could always introduce me to your friend to convince me.'

'Now?' grinned Tony.

'Why not?' answered Nigel. He was getting annoyed with Tony's obvious enjoyment and I-know-better-than-you smiles.

'I can't,' said Tony calmly, 'because vampires don't get up till after sunset, and it's still daytime at the moment.'

'So why did you say you'd arranged to meet him, then?'

'Well, I had to start this nonsense somewhere, didn't I?'

Nigel was so surprised that for a moment he just looked at Tony without saying a word. Then he turned puce in the face, and his voice cracked with anger. 'You – you little creep! Just shut up about your vampires! It's all fairy tales anyway!'

'But you believed me!' laughed Tony.

'I certainly did not!' raged Nigel.

Tony just went on grinning.

'And anyhow,' finished Nigel, 'I'm off home!' He turned on his heels and stamped off.

At that moment, an idea occurred to Tony. What if Nigel were to come on Wednesday, and not Rudolph... but not as Nigel, as Rudolph... that was it! The answer! His parents would stop going on at him, because they would think they had met Rudolph at last!

'Ni-igel!' called Tony as loudly as he could, and ran off after him. 'Wait!'

CHAPTER NINE
Anna the Toothless

Tony was already asleep when something tapped gently on his window. Blinking his eyes sleepily, he could only make out through the drawn curtains the outlines of two dark shapes crouching on the windowsill. It had to be vampires, for who else could be outside in the middle of the night, tapping on a window on the sixth floor! But he wondered why there were two. Rudolph always came alone. Perhaps it was a trap! Perhaps Rudolph's family had found out where he, Tony, lived! But Rudolph would surely have warned him if that had happened. No, Tony decided, it was far more likely just to be Rudolph outside – but who on earth had he brought with him?

The tapping came again, this time more impatiently. Tony tiptoed over to the window and peeped through the curtains. He recognised the little vampire, with his cloak wrapped tightly round him, and by his side a second, much smaller vampire, who was also wearing a black cloak.

Tony heard a whisper from outside. 'It's me, Rudolph!' His heart beating loudly, Tony drew the curtains to one side, and there sat a girl-vampire! He was so astonished that for a moment he remained speechless, rooted to the spot.

'Open up!' called Rudolph, sliding restlessly backwards and forwards on the windowsill. Tony quickly opened the window, and the two vampires slipped noiselessly into the room.

'My sister,' said Rudolph indicating the girl vampire. 'Anna the Toothless!' Her face was small and very white, with pink eyes and a round, little mouth.

She smiled shyly at Tony, and two red spots appeared on her cheeks as she rounded on her brother. 'You shouldn't introduce me as "Anna the Toothless",' she complained. 'For a start, they are growing, and anyway, you didn't have any either when you were my age!'

'She's the only one in our family who drinks milk!' giggled the vampire.

'Not any more!' said Anna defiantly.

'She was absolutely determined to meet you,' went on the vampire.

Anna's face turned an even deeper shade of red. 'So?' she said, glaring at her brother. 'Isn't that allowed?' Turning to Tony, she continued: 'In fact, I wanted to see your books. He –' and she pointed at her brother – 'told me that you had masses and masses.' She went over to the bookshelf, and picked one out. 'What about this one? *Twelve Chilling Vampire Tales*. Will you lend it to me?'

'Er – OK,' said Tony.

'Thank you,' she said smiling, and tucked the book under her cloak, at the same time throwing a triumphant look in the direction of her brother.

She would really look quite pretty for a vampire,

thought Tony, if only her face were not quite so pale, and if she did not have those dark rings under her eyes...but what did it matter? As if he was interested in girl-vampires!

Meanwhile, Rudolph had made himself comfortable at Tony's desk, and was looking around inquisitively. 'By the way,' he asked. 'Where's that other cloak of mine?'

Tony had been dreading that question. 'Well,' he began, noticing out of the corner of one eye that Anna was leafing through one book after another. 'It's not here, exactly.'

'Not here?' questioned the vampire.

'I've lent it to someone.'

'*Lent* it?' The vampire looked angry and suspicious. 'Why?'

'Um, well, my parents...' He tailed off, realising for the first time that his parents were asleep in the next room. He continued in a whisper, 'My parents wanted me to ask you round.'

'Me?' cried the vampire in amazement.

'Yes, you,' said Tony, 'because I'd told them so much about you. That's why I had to go to the cemetery with the cloak today.'

'To the cemetery?' repeated the vampire. 'Why didn't we see each other?'

Even Anna pricked up her ears. 'I didn't see you either,' she said.

'It was in the daytime,' explained Tony.

'Pity,' sighed Anna.

'Anyway, when I got to the cemetery, this guy from school –' Rudolph didn't have to be told they were friends, after all – 'turned up, and suddenly I had a brilliant idea. Nigel could pretend to be you!'

'How'd he do that?' asked Rudolph.

'Well, I'd introduce him as "Rudolph Sackville-Bagg"!'

'Would it work?' asked the vampire nervously.

'Sure. My parents have never met Nigel. And anyway, I told him all about it.'

'*All* about it?' asked the vampire in a meaningful voice, looking rather dangerously at Tony.

Tony hastened to reassure him. 'Of course, nothing about the vault, or about your relatives. In any case, he doesn't believe in vampires!'

'That's lucky,' said Rudolph, and breathed a sigh of relief.

'But Tony believes in us!' warbled Anna, and gave a little skip and a jump.

'Leave off!' hissed the vampire.

Anna looked downcast. 'Can't you stop getting at me?' she said. 'What will Tony think?'

'I should think it's too late to worry about that!' teased the vampire. 'He must have realised by now that you're just a silly little baby who thinks he's a hero!'

'Wh-a-at did you say?' screeched Anna, marching furiously over to Rudolph. 'If you dare say that again . . .' And she shook her tiny fist in his face.

'OK, OK,' relented Rudolph. 'I'm sorry.'

Mollified by this, Anna gave Tony a heartfelt look and returned to her place on the bed.

'So when do I get my cloak back?' resumed the vampire.

'Y-your cloak?' stammered Tony. He was still watching the door anxiously, knowing that it might be flung open at any moment. Usually his parents woke up at the slightest cough! Even quiet music disturbed them, and already Tony had had some explaining to do about his radio. Anna had just that moment discovered it. She was turning the knobs curiously, and before Tony could do anything, raucous pop music blared out across the room.

'Oh no!' groaned Tony, but too late. The door of his parents' bedroom had opened.

'Quick!' he hissed, and switched off the radio. 'Hide!'

Rudolph and Anna hardly had time to crawl under Tony's bed before his mother appeared in the doorway. Her face looked grey and crumpled, and her hair stood out from her head in wild ringlets.

'Tony,' she said sleepily, 'how often have I told you...?'

'I know, I know,' interrupted Tony. 'I'm sorry.' His mother gave him one of her reproachful looks and shook her head, then turned as if to go. But then she stopped. 'Tony,' she said, 'there's a funny smell in here.'

'I can't smell anything,' said Tony innocently.

'I can. Something smells...mouldy.'

'Mouldy?' repeated Tony, stationing himself in front of the bed.

'*Something smells in here*,' said his mother emphatically. She went slowly round the room, sniffing suspiciously in each corner. Luckily, she didn't look under the bed, but came to a standstill in the middle of the room.

'When did you last have a bath. Tony?' she asked.

'Yesterday,' said Tony, ignoring the soft giggle that came from under the bed.

'There's nothing to laugh about,' said his mother sternly. 'You know you ought to have a bath every day.' Sniffing indignantly, she added, 'You smell as

if you need one!' There was another titter from under the bed.

'OK, laugh!' said his mother crossly. 'It won't seem so funny in the morning. I'll see to it that you wash, my boy.' With this last retort, she stalked out, shutting the door behind her with a determined click, and Tony made sure he heard his parents' door close too before he sank onto his bed in relief.

'By the skin of our teeth!' he breathed.

'What's that about teeth?' asked Anna, wriggling out from under the bed.

'Just a figure of speech,' said Rudolph condescendingly. 'But of course, babies can't be expected to understand.'

'Huh!' sniffed Anna, and stuck out her tongue.

'We must be off,' announced the vampire.

'Already?' asked Anna sadly.

'Now,' growled the vampire, and jumped onto the windowsill. 'It'll soon be light. Come on!'

Anna looked pleadingly at Tony. 'May I come again?' she asked.

'Er, of course,' said Tony, rather taken aback.

'Great!' she gurgled, and with a single bound was out through the window, looking for all the world like a rather large butterfly hovering outside.

'What about the cloak?' asked the vampire. 'When do I get it back?'

'Wednesday,' answered Tony.

'OK,' said the vampire, and added softly, 'You see, it's not even mine. I got it out of Uncle Theodore's coffin!'

'The one with the woo...' Wooden stake, was what Tony had been about to say, but he had stopped himself just in time. He remembered only too well how vampires feel about wooden stakes! But in any case, Rudolph had missed Tony's last words...and had already sailed off into the night.

As long as Nigel remembers the cloak on Wednesday, all will be well, Tony just had time to think before he fell asleep.

CHAPTER TEN
Nigel's Great Performance

'Your Rudolph isn't the most punctual of friends,' said Tony's mother on Wednesday. The clock said half past four, and Nigel still had not arrived.

'Never mind,' said Tony. 'It doesn't matter.'

'It certainly does matter,' contradicted his mother. 'The tea's getting cold.'

Tony thought the table looked as if she was expecting a state visit! All the best china was out, and the silver spoons and even the candlesticks. A special cake had been baked that very afternoon for the occasion, and it smelt delicious; there were Tony's favourite cream buns as well, and the expensive chocolate biscuits with the chewy fillings, which his mother never bought for everyday tea.

'Shouldn't you ring him up?' suggested his mother, and before Tony could answer, she had got out the telephone directory. She ran down the column of names with her finger. 'Sack Sackerman – Sackmore – Sackstone – Sackwood. There isn't a Sackville-Bagg,' she said, and looked questioningly at Tony.

'I could have told you that,' said Tony.

'Did you know they don't have a phone?' asked his mother.

'Well, I didn't know, but I guessed they might.' said Tony evasively.

'Why?' His mother was all ears now. But at that very moment, the doorbell rang.

Tony leapt up in relief. 'That must be him!' he said, and ran to the door. I hope it really is Nigel, he thought. What on earth am I going to say to Mum and Dad if he's left me in the lurch?

But it was Nigel. At first, Tony could hardly recognise him in his dark trousers, black shirt, and swathed, according to instructions, in the famous cloak.

'Hello!' he grinned. 'How do I look?'

Tony looked quickly over his shoulder. 'Ssh!' he whispered. 'We mustn't give the game away.' Out loud, he said, 'Hi Rudolph! Come on in!'

Mum appeared in the hall. 'How nice,' she cooed. 'Hello, Rudolph. I'm very pleased to meet you.'

'Good afternoon,' said Nigel, making a low bow.

'You know your way around the flat already,' said Tony's mother, watching Nigel closely, 'but we've never met. Once you hid in the cupboard, and then when tea was ready, you'd disappeared.' Nigel just stood and grinned. 'Anyway,' went on Tony's mother. 'What do you think of your cloak?'

'The cloak?' repeated Nigel. 'It's great.'

'Haven't you noticed anything different about it?'

Nigel looked puzzled. 'What sort of thing?'

'The holes, of course,' laughed Tony's mother. 'I've darned them.'

'Oh – er, yes – thank you very much,' murmured Nigel.

'Tony said you didn't want them mended.'

'Really? Why?'

Tony came to the rescue. 'Because then it wouldn't look like a real vampire costume,' he chipped in.

'Oh, yes.' Nigel looked as if the penny had just dropped. 'My vampire costume. Well, Mrs Peasbody, it's just that it looks more spooky with holes in it.'

Tony's mother smiled. 'Come along in,' she said. They were over the first hurdle, thought Tony. Nigel wasn't bad, he'd give him that. In fact, for the three pounds it was going to cost him, the performance was cheap at the price!

'I hope you are enjoying your tea,' said Tony's mother, when they were all sitting round the table.

'Mmm, thank you,' mumbled Nigel, who had already devoured a quarter of the cake and was now cramming a cream bun in his mouth.

'I really didn't know what to make for you,' smiled Tony's mother. 'Tony had told me such extraordinary stories about what you liked to eat.' She poured herself a cup of tea. 'He said you only ate or drank one thing, and that we didn't have any of it in the house.'

'How strange,' said Nigel.

'But I can see now that you've got a very good appetite,' said Tony's mother, looking pleased.

Nigel nodded and took another cream bun. 'I've always liked eating,' he said through a mouthful of crumbs. 'My mum always says: "Nigel, you'll eat us out of house and home!"'

'What does she call you?' asked Tony's mother in astonishment. 'Nigel?'

'Er, yes, that's my second name,' said Nigel quickly. 'Rudolph Nigel Sackville–' He hesitated, and looked desperately at Tony.

Sackville-Bagg! Tony's lips silently mouthed the name.

'Sackville-Wagg!' said Nigel firmly, misunderstanding Tony's prompting.

Tony's mother was even more confused. 'What?' she said.

'I mean Sackville-Bang,' Nigel tried again.

'Oh, you're just trying to make a fool of me!' laughed Tony's mother.

'No, no, Mrs Peasbody, of course not,' Nigel assured her, reaching for another cream bun.

'Hey!' protested Tony. 'Leave some for other people!'

'Tony!' rebuked his mother. 'You shouldn't speak to your guest like that!'

'I don't know who's behaving like a guest round here!' stormed Tony. 'Guests don't guzzle their way straight through three cream buns!'

'Course they don't,' agreed Nigel peaceably, taking the last one. 'They eat four!'

Tony was speechless. He'd invited Nigel to tea, and now the pig was devouring cakes as if he hadn't eaten for a week. What on earth was his mum going

to think? 'Rudolph, I think it's time you were going,' he said in a strangled voice.

Nigel did not agree. He grinned unashamedly, and proceeded to pile his plate with chocolate biscuits. 'Why should I?'

'Because...' began Tony, but he was interrupted by the sound of the doorbell.

'That'll be Dad,' said Tony's mother, getting up.

'Dad?' asked Tony, sounding surprised.

'He arranged to come home early,' explained his mother.

Once she had left the room. Tony rounded on Nigel. 'If you think you can come here and do just what you like...' he hissed, but Nigel interrupted.

'Hey, steady on,' he said with mock concern.

'I'll ... I'll ...' But before he could find the appropriate threat, his father came into the room.

'Hello, Rudolph,' he said.

Nigel half rose from his chair. 'Afternoon.'

'So, at last we've got the chance to get to know you,' said Tony's father, sitting down.

He doesn't even notice me, thought Tony grumpily. But then, I'm not a guest!

'You're the one who thinks it's always Hallowe'en,' said Tony's father conversationally.

'I–I do?' asked Nigel.

'Tony's told us that you're always dressed for a Hallowe'en party.'

'Ow!' cried Nigel, as Tony landed a sharp kick on his shin from under the table. 'Er, yes, I suppose I am.'

'How do you work it in the summer?' pursued Tony's father.

Nigel was at a loss at this, so said nothing and took another biscuit instead.

'You must have a special party?' smiled Tony's father.

'Perhaps he doesn't want to talk about it,' suggested Tony hastily.

'Quite.' Nigel nodded.

Tony's father pointed to the cloak and remarked, 'You've even got your costume on today. Are you going to pretend it's Hallowe'en tonight?'

'Not tonight,' said Nigel hurriedly. 'Tomorrow, probably. Now, I really must be going.'

'So soon?' asked Tony's mother, appearing from the kitchen with a fresh pot of tea.

'I'm afraid so,' said Nigel. 'I've got to get some things ready.'

'What sort of things?' asked Tony's father. 'Do you have to polish your vampire teeth? Or have you got a set of those rubber fangs?'

'Rubber fangs?' Nigel was completely lost.

'Yes. All the best vampire costumes have rubber fangs to go with them. If you don't have two pointed teeth, you're not a proper vampire!'

Nigel had gone pale. He even seemed to have lost his appetite, for he stood up, murmuring, 'I must be off.'

'Goodbye,' called Tony's astonished parents.

'Bye,' said Nigel.

Tony went with him to the door. When they were out of earshot, he asked, 'Why did you get up so suddenly?'

'Why?' sneered Nigel. 'Because I don't like being squeezed like a lemon, that's why. Apart from that, I suddenly realised that I'd met your father.'

'No!' gasped Tony. 'Where?'

'My dad sits in the same office as yours at work.'

'Did he recognise you?' asked Tony.

'I hope not,' said Nigel. 'Look what I look like!' He grinned. 'Bye, then, Tony.'

'Wait!' cried Tony. 'The cloak!'

'Oh yes, this old rag,' said Nigel, pulling it off. 'Here you are, I'm not wearing that again!'

Tony quickly rolled it up and stuck it under his pullover. 'Bye, Rudolph!' he said, loudly enough for his parents to hear, and shut the door. Thank goodness that was over. Now all he had to do was hide the cloak. He tiptoed across the hall. The door of the living room was open, and he could hear his parents talking quietly. No doubt they were still at the table discussing Rudolph!

'Tony!' called his mother. 'Is that you?'

'Just coming,' he answered and slipped into his room.

'What's the matter?' asked his mother.

'Nothing,' replied Tony, stuffing the cloak under his bed. 'Here I am.'

As he had guessed, his parents were sitting at the table with rather puzzled expressions on their faces. 'Well?' asked Tony bluntly. 'What did you think of him?'

'He wasn't very talkative,' said his mother.

'He never is,' said Tony.

'And I've met better behaved boys,' she went on.

'So've I,' agreed Tony, thinking wistfully of the cream buns.

'In fact, I can't think why he is such a good pal of yours,' announced his mother.

Nor me, thought Tony to himself. Out loud, he asked: 'What about you, Dad. What did you think?'

'Well, I didn't see much of him. But I got the feeling I'd seen him somewhere before.'

'Mmm,' Tony could not resist a smile. 'I wonder.'

'Do you think I have?' asked his father.

'Of course not.' Tony had never looked so innocent. He felt quite elated. Everything had gone according to plan. And it was highly unlikely that his father would ever remember where he had met Nigel – at least, he hoped not!

CHAPTER ELEVEN
At Dusk

'Would you mind if I went to my room?' asked Tony politely.

'Of course not,' said his mother. 'But why?'

'I've got something to do for school,' said Tony. This was not exactly true, but it was always a good excuse, and one to which his parents never raised any objection. Once in his room, Tony threw himself down on his bed. Nigel didn't half fancy himself, he thought. He was, of course, very grateful that Nigel had played the game at all, and what's more, he'd done it very well: his parents hadn't suspected a thing! But the play-acting during tea! Still, at least now his parents knew who Rudolph was, and wouldn't go on at him any more about meeting his friend . . . after all, they'd had an eyeful of him that afternoon!

Tony must have fallen asleep, for when he opened his eyes, it was already getting dark. All was quiet in the flat. Perhaps his parents had gone out? Tony went to the door and listened carefully. There was not a sound to be heard. If his parents were at home, the television was bound to be on, or at least the radio, and sometimes they even talked to each other! Tony decided they must have gone out for a walk.

He was thirsty, and suddenly remembered the chocolate milkshake his mother had made for Nigel.

Perhaps there was some left. An exploration of the fridge revealed a piece of the cake, but no milkshake, only orange juice. Tony had to be content with that, and taking the cake with him, he went back to his room. As he crossed the hall, he noticed a strange, rather mouldy smell, which had not been there before. It was not the cloak; that just smelt of old clothes. And it could not be Rudolph, because he always smelt rather singed! Was it one of the other vampires? After all, he had left his window open...

He opened his bedroom door cautiously and asked: 'Is anyone there?' A low chuckle was the only answer.

'Rudolph?' he called into the gloom.

'No!' came the reply, followed by a high-pitched girlish giggle.

'Anna!' guessed Tony.

'Right!' The lamp by Tony's bed was switched on, and its light revealed Anna sitting on the bed, looking pleased with herself. She looked different: her hair, which on Sunday had hung in wild tangles down to her shoulders, had been brushed till it gleamed. Her eyes shone, and excitement had brought colour to her deathly-pale cheeks. What on earth was she doing here, wondered Tony. He hoped she was not on the prowl. Anna must have guessed his thoughts, because she began to laugh. 'Have you forgotten I'm called Anna the Toothless?' she asked.

Tony felt foolish. Unable to think of anything else to say, he held out the glass and asked: 'Do you like orange juice?'

'She shook her head. 'No. But I'd love some milk.'

'Wait a second,' said Tony, and a moment later he returned with a glass of milk.

'Thanks,' she smiled, and drank it with little sips, watching him over the rim of her glass in a way that made him feel very uncomfortable.

'Er,' he coughed. 'Would you like to borrow another book?'

'No thanks,' she said.

'Oh. Er, well, then why have you come?'

'I just wanted to see you,' she said with a beaming smile. 'Do you mind?'

'N-no,' he stammered.

'How do I look today?' she asked.

'V-very nice.' This was becoming ridiculous!

'Do you really think so?' she said happily, smoothing down her hair. 'It was really very difficult. I hadn't combed my hair for seventy-five years!' Her expression changed as she plucked at her cloak. 'I hate this old thing,' she grumbled. 'Do you know, I never minded before what I looked like. But now I think you'd like me better in pretty clothes, wouldn't you?'

'I don't know,' said Tony. 'You couldn't fly without your cloak.'

'It's so unfair,' she sighed. 'Normal girls can wear what they like, it's only vampire girls who have to dress in crummy old things like this.' She bit her lip and seemed to be thinking. 'May I ask you something?' she said finally.

'Of course,' said Tony, rather surprised.

'What do you think of vampires?'

Tony wasn't prepared for this. 'Oh-er, they're great!' he answered.

'And ... vampire girls?'

'Vampire girls?' he hedged. 'I only know one!'

'Well, what do you think of me?' she tittered.

'You're OK,' he muttered, and felt himself blush.

Her face fell. 'Only OK?' she said. 'I think you're much, much nicer than OK!' She stopped suddenly, and looked as if she was going to cry.

What on earth was he going to do? The whole conversation had got out of hand, thought Tony, who would much rather talk of less dangerous subjects.

'Where is Rudolph?' he asked hurriedly.

'You only ever think about Rudolph,' she sighed.

'Not at all,' said Tony. 'But he is going to pick up the cloak tonight?'

'Was going to,' she said with a sniff.

'Isn't he coming, then?'

'No. He can't. He's ill.'

'Ill?' Tony sounded worried. 'It wasn't ... the Nightwatchmen?' he asked, with a catch in his voice.

'No,' she said. 'Blood poisoning.'

'Blood poisoning?' echoed Tony. That sounded a very serious disease. 'Where is he?'

'In his coffin with a temperature,' she replied.

Tony did not know what to say. Poor Rudolph was lying alone in his coffin with no one to look after him. When *he* was ill, his parents sent for the doctor and brought him grapes and Lucozade to make him feel better.

'Could we go and see him?' he asked.

'See him?' giggled Anna. 'And what if my parents saw *you*? Or my grandparents? Or my aunt? Or my brother?'

'Yes...er, well, perhaps we'd better not,' agreed Tony, whose hair began to stand on end at the mere mention of the other vampires. 'Is he very ill?'

'Are you worried he might die?' asked Anna. Tony nodded. 'Well, forget it! He's dead already, remember!'

Tony had not thought of that, but he did not think that it made much difference. 'Even so, he must be feeling rotten,' he said. 'We ought to look after him.'

'What does "look after" mean?' Anna asked. She had never heard that expression before.

'Looking after someone means you go and see them, and play games with them, and read them a story and make them laugh.' At least, that was what happened whenever he was ill. Tony wasn't sure what you did with vampires!

'No one looks after us,' said Anna. 'My family are either all asleep in their coffins or out and...well, you know all about that.' She sighed. 'Anyway, nobody has any time for us. Nobody has ever read me a story or played a game with me.'

Poor Anna, thought Tony. It must be really tough being a vampire kid. He always thought his parents took little enough notice of him, but he had a fantastic time compared to a vampire!

'We could look after Rudolph, as long as your family isn't there,' he suggested.

'Supposing one of them comes home early?' asked Anna.

Tony waved his hand nonchalantly. 'That's hardly likely,' he said. 'Anyway, I've already been to the vault once.'

'What!' exclaimed Anna. 'You've already been there?'

'Yeah, with Rudolph,' said Tony.

'And no one found out?'

'No. Aunt Dorothy nearly did, but I got into Rudolph's coffin just in time!'

Anna breathed a sigh of relief. 'Aunt Dorothy's the worst,' she said. 'She once had a go at me, even though I'm a vampire too!'

'Ugh!' Tony could not stop himself. He felt his throat gingerly as he remembered Aunt Dorothy's strident voice echoing around the vault.

'But she's nearly always out the longest,' said Anna soothingly. 'She's the greediest, you see. So – when are we off?'

Tony seemed to have lost his earlier enthusiasm. 'Do you really think we should?'

'Yeah. Come on! You said yourself that we ought to be looking after Rudolph.'

'OK. If you're sure.'

'Come on,' she urged. 'You've got the other cloak.' She jumped up and down on the windowsill with impatience. 'Rudolph will be surprised,' she chuckled.

'I just hope it's all right,' said Tony, joining her on the sill with the cloak. And away they flew.

CHAPTER TWELVE
First Aid

The wall of the cemetery was already in sight. The sky was clear, the moon shining brightly, and consequently the cemetery looked much less spooky and mysterious to Tony than it had the Sunday before. Perhaps it was just that this was his third visit, he thought, as he followed Anna over the wall and landed in the grass on the other side.

'The entrance is just over there,' Anna whispered, 'but we must wait to make sure everything's quiet.'

Tony nodded. 'I know,' he said. 'The Nightwatchman.'

'Ssh,' she hissed.

Tony looked around at the tilted gravestones, almost overgrown by the long grass, the rusty old crosses sticking up out of the undergrowth, and the shadowy mass of the yew tree, under which lay the entrance to the vault.

Anna was straining her ears to catch the slightest sound. After a while, she stood up. 'OK,' she said. 'We can go.'

'Why don't you, er, go first?' suggested Tony, who suddenly felt rather sick, like you do when you have not eaten for a whole day.

Anna looked surprised. 'Why? I promise there won't be anyone else in the vault apart from Rudolph.'

'But you could just make quite sure,' insisted Tony. What if Aunt Dorothy had had another fainting fit? Or if one of the others had stayed behind to look after Rudolph? Tony shuddered at the thought of coming face to face with Thelma the Thirsty!

'Oh, all right,' said Anna. 'I'll have a look. But you must keep hidden.' She vanished down into the hole, and Tony crept deeper into the shadows.

At that very moment, he heard soft footsteps. They sounded quite a way off, but in the stillness that enveloped the graveyard, there could be no doubt of their reality. An icy shudder ran through him. It couldn't be Nigel, could it? But he would never have been able to follow them from the ground. No, there was only one explanation: the Nightwatchman!

By now, Tony could make out the figure of a man. He was quite small, and he was moving swiftly but carefully, his head turning questioningly from this side to that. As he came nearer, Tony could make out a grey, wrinkled face, with a pointed nose and bright, restless little eyes, all of which made him look rather like a rat. Then Tony's gaze was riveted to something else: out of the pocket of his overalls poked an enormous hammer and some sharp wooden stakes!

Tony hardly dared breathe. The deep shadow of the yew tree hid him perfectly, so he felt he was fairly safe, but Anna...at any moment, she would pop her head up to call him, and the Nightwatchman was

only a metre away! He had already turned those piercing eyes onto the darkness under the yew tree!

Tony saw the stone at the entrance to the vault begin to move, and suddenly he had an idea. He, picked up a largish stone from the ground, and lobbed it as far as he could away from the yew tree. The stone landed heavily some way away, and, like a hound on the scent, the Nightwatchman hurried off in the direction of the noise, baying: 'Now I've got you!' Tony watched him start rummaging around in the undergrowth, brandishing the hammer and one of the wooden stakes. Tony raced over to Anna, and slid down into the vault, pulling the stone over the entrance after him.

'Phew!' he gulped, leaning against the cool stone wall. 'That was close!'

'What was?' asked Anna.

'The Nightwatchman,' said Tony, still out of breath. 'He nearly caught you moving the stone!'

'The Nightwatchman?' gasped Anna. 'Did you see him?'

'Yeah – but he didn't see me.'

'Where is he now?'

Tony grinned. 'Looking for a stone!'

'What?'

'I chucked a stone to distract him, and now he's on the wrong trail,' explained Tony.

Anna breathed a sigh of relief. 'Don't you think he looks like a rat?'

'Mmm,' agreed Tony. 'Hideous.'

'I quite agree,' giggled Anna. 'We vampires look really quite sweet in comparison. Do you know what his name is? Mr McRookery!'

'No!' laughed Tony.

'It is!' Anna grinned delightedly and hopped from one foot-to the other chanting: 'Silly Mr McRookery! You don't know where us vampires be!'

A rasping cough from the vault interrupted them.

'Rudolph!' cried Tony, 'How is he?'

'Him?' scoffed Anna. 'He's all right. He's already up and about. But now Gruesome Gregory's got it.'

'Gruesome Gregory?' Who on earth was Gruesome Gregory? Of course, their elder brother.

'Does he know that I'm…?'

'Of course,' nodded Anna. 'But don't worry. We vampire kids stick together!'

'He…er…won't do anything to me?'

'No!' smiled Anna. 'At least, not with us around.'

They went down the steps. One candle was burning, and by its light, they could see Rudolph sitting in his coffin reading, while in the coffin next to him a bigger, stronger vampire was tossing and turning. Rudolph looked up from his book and laid a finger across his lips. 'He's asleep,' he whispered, and motioned to them to come and sit on the edge of his coffin.

'What's wrong with him?' asked Tony.

''Flu,' replied Rudolph, 'and no wonder, out in the damp air every night.'

Tony looked furtively at the slumbering form. A certain similarity with Rudolph was unmistakable, but Gruesome Gregory's face was paler and the hollows of his eyes even more pronounced. 'He looks ill,' said Tony.

'Mmm,' nodded Rudolph. 'Drained of blood, poor thing.'

A deep growl came from Gregory, making Tony shrink back in fright. He hoped Anna had been right about how harmless her elder brother was!

'I wanted to come and see you, Rudolph,' he explained, 'but since you're better…'

'You're not going already?' cried Anna.

'I–I ought to get back home,' said Tony. 'I haven't got my key.' He had to get out before Gregory woke up!

But already, it was too late. Gruesome Gregory opened his eyes. He sat up, grumbling, and stared at Tony. 'Who is this?' he asked in a menacing voice.

'Oh, Greg,' crooned Anna. 'This is Tony. Don't you remember, we told you about him?'

'Oh yes,' said Gregory, sounding disappointed. 'Tony. I'm hungry.'

'You can go out again tomorrow,' soothed Anna. Gregory yawned. His mouth opened so wide that Tony could see the rows of gleaming pointed teeth; his eye teeth were over an inch long! Tony shivered. He wished he could get out of the vault, but of course the worst thing he could do would be to show he was frightened: that would make him easy prey!

Gregory was smiling now. 'Don't come too close to me,' he said. 'You might catch something you don't want!'

'Er – quite,' said Tony, who had no intention of getting any closer to Gregory. 'Perhaps it would be better if I went home.'

'Why?' sniggered Gregory. 'Don't you like it here?'

'Y-yes,' Tony protested, stuttering. 'Of course I do. It's just that I don't want to get 'flu.'

'Let's play Ludo!' proposed Gregory, and he pulled a long, slim box out of his coffin.

'Yes, let's!' agreed Anna excitedly. 'Come on, Rudolph, help me set up the table.'

They brought a little coffin over from the wall and turned it over, so that it made a perfect table between Gregory's coffin and the one next door. Gregory set out the board with the counters on it, and they all gathered round, Tony still rather hesitant.

'I'll be black,' said Gregory.

'Bags I red!' said Anna.

'What colour do you want?' Rudolph asked Tony.

'Oh, er, yellow,' said Tony.

'Who's going to start?' asked Anna.

'Tony,' said Gregory. 'Guests are always allowed to start.' He pushed the dice over to Tony, who shook it and threw. It was a four.

'Bad luck,' said Gregory with a gloating grin. 'You have to throw a six to start.'

Now it was Rudolph's turn, which gave Tony a chance to look at the board properly. It looked like a normal one, except that the 'counters' had pointed teeth!

'How did you get the game?' he whispered to Anna.

'Uncle Theo found it for us,' she replied.

'Found it?' asked Tony in disbelief. How could anyone just 'find' a game?

'Well,' she tittered, 'perhaps it would be better to call it 'booty'!'

Gregory had just had his turn, and had thrown a two. 'Unfair!' he grumbled, and flung the dice away in a temper. Rudolph ran after it and brought it back to the table. Now it was Anna's turn. She threw

carefully, and it landed just at the edge of the board: a six!

'Doesn't count!' shouted Gregory. 'Cocked dice!'

'It isn't!' stormed Anna. 'It's flat on the board!' Before she could pick up the dice to throw again, Gregory brought his fist crashing down on the coffin, so that the dice flew up in the air. Anna went crimson with fury. 'You can't *ever* lose, can you?' she fumed.

Gregory looked offended, but did not say anything. He lay back in his coffin with dignity, and shut his eyes. Rudolph shrugged his shoulders and began to look for the scattered pieces of the game, which he carefully put back in the box. Meanwhile, a contented snoring rose from the coffin.

'Is he asleep?' asked Tony.

Anna shook her head. 'He's only pretending. But mind you don't disturb him!'

'He's got quite a temper,' whispered Tony.

'Ssh,' said Anna. 'Don't get him worked up again. It's just a sign of puberty.'

'Of what?' asked Tony.

'Growing up,' explained Anna.

'Oh, I see.' Tony thought of Gregory's grating voice, which seemed to change pitch constantly. 'His voice is breaking, then?'

'Exactly,' said Anna, 'and that's why he's so moody and quick tempered. But the worst thing is that he'll never grow out of it. He died in puberty, and there he'll stay.'

At that moment, the stone at the entrance of the vault began to move. Gregory went on pretending to be asleep, but Rudolph was rooted to the spot, his eyes fixed in horror on the entrance. Anna pulled Tony to one side and whispered: 'You must hide!'

'Where?' gasped Tony.

'In one of the coffins!'

'I'll go in Rudolph's, then,' stammered Tony. At least he knew that one, and had managed to survive the revolting smell once already. He dreaded to think what horrors the other coffins might hold in store.

Anna helped him to clamber in, and then shut the lid. It was not a moment too soon: already there was the sound of hurrying feet coming down the steps, and a voice, which Tony recognised only too well, called: 'Drat and botheration! This could only happen to me!'

'What's happened. Aunt Dorothy?'

'My false teeth!' she complained. 'I must have left them behind in my coffin.'

Tony heard her clattering across the vault.

'There they are!' she said in relief. 'Imagine if I'd lost them for good!' Apparently she had put them in place by now, for these last words sounded much more distinct.

'Right, I'll be off again,' she declared. Then she stopped. 'Rudolph, why aren't you in your coffin?'

'I'm feeling much better, Aunt,' explained Rudolph.

'Nonsense! I'm sure you're not,' insisted Aunt Dorothy. 'What would your mother say? Get back into your coffin immediately!'

Tony's heart nearly stopped beating.

Footsteps came nearer, the lid opened and a figure clambered into the coffin. 'You see?' hissed Rudolph. 'Plenty of room for two!' Out loud he called: 'Good night, everyone!' and closed the lid. They heard Aunt Dorothy clatter back up the steps, and a minute later, Anna gave the all clear.

However, all that came from the coffin was a low moan. Anna opened the lid anxiously, and saw Rudolph leaning over Tony, whose eyes were tightly closed. She called out in alarm: 'Rudolph! You wouldn't hurt Tony!' Her cry woke Tony, who gave a yelp when he saw the vampire.

Slowly, Rudolph lifted his head. 'Have you all gone crazy?' he said calmly. 'I was only giving Tony artificial respiration.'

'Artificial respiration?' echoed Tony suspiciously, gingerly feeling his neck; but there was not the slightest trace of a bite, and no blood either.

'You had fainted,' explained Rudolph, 'and I thought I could...'

'Oh, you and your first aid course!' scoffed Anna.

'I'm going,' said Tony limply. His legs felt like cotton wool. He sat up slowly, and climbed out of the coffin.

'Poor Tony,' Anna said, 'I'll take you home.'

'Thanks,' mumbled Tony.

Together they climbed the steps. They had nearly reached the top, when Rudolph bobbed up next to them. He looked apologetic. 'I'm sorry. Tony,' he said shamefacedly. 'I-I only wanted to help you. You don't really believe I'd...'

'No, of course not,' said Tony, holding out his hand. 'It's forgotten.'

'I am glad,' breathed Rudolph. 'I thought you might have had enough of us!'

'Come on, Tony!' called Anna. 'We can go now.'

'OK, then,' said Tony, turning in the narrow passage. 'See you on Saturday,' He never heard Rudolph's reply, for Anna had taken his hand, and pulled him up into the fresh air.

CHAPTER THIRTEEN
Anna's Idea

The clean night air restored Tony once more to his senses. He breathed in great gulps of it, and stretched his stiff limbs. Anna watched him, smiling.

'Was it that bad?' she asked.

'In the coffin, you mean? No.' At least it was over now, and he was safely out of the clutches of Gregory and Aunt Dorothy. 'It was just a bit narrow,' he explained. 'And rather – stuffy.'

'Stuffy?' giggled Anna. 'Well, what do you expect? We can't ever air them, exactly. And as for these old cloaks...'

She broke off, looking worriedly around her as if something had just occurred to her. 'We ought to get going,' she whispered. 'Who knows if old McRookery is lurking around the place.'

'Have you seen him?'

'No. But it's best not to take chances.' She took off into the air, Tony following unsteadily.

'There was something I wanted to ask you,' she said. 'Are there any love stories about vampires?

'Love stories?' Tony thought for a moment. 'I can't think of any.'

They flew along together without speaking. After a while, Anna said dreamily: 'I read one once which had a happy ending.'

'Oh?' said Tony. 'What happened?'

'Well, the boy ended up as a vampire too, and they both lived happily ever after.'

'Yuck!' said Tony. 'I don't call that a happy ending!'

'Don't you?' Anna looked at him with wide, imploring eyes. 'Not even if it was with me?'

Tony was aware he would have to be careful. This was dangerous ground again. 'Well, I can't ever become a vampire, you see.'

'Why not?' asked Anna. 'If I...' She paused, realising that it was perhaps not quite the right moment to initiate Tony into the finer points of how to become a vampire. It might scare him off!

'Er, you see, as soon as I get my teeth, I will be able to...'

'I do *not* want to become a vampire!' interrupted Tony.

'You don't?' Anna could not believe it.

'No!' he said emphatically, irritated that she should presume he would. 'And what's more, I haven't the slightest intention of becoming one!' This was going a bit too far!

He flew on ahead, without deigning to look at her. It was not until he heard a sob from behind that he turned round.

'Y-you don't l-like me!' she sniffed. 'Y-you've got another g-girlfriend.'

'I haven't!' insisted Tony. 'I promise you that!'

'Really?'

'Yeah.'

She sighed with relief and wiped her eyes with the back of her hand. 'It doesn't matter if you're not a vampire,' she said, 'as long as we're friends.' She began to smile again.

'We're almost there,' said Tony hurriedly, even though in fact there was another quarter of a mile to go. Why did Anna always have to start these embarrassing conversations? 'I think I can see the lights,' he continued, beginning to fly more quickly. He would not normally be in such a hurry to get home, but with Anna on his heels, it was a different matter. He could not bear to think of what other questions she might dream up to ask him!

In the living room, his parents had switched on the television. Tony only hoped they had not noticed his absence, as then he could simply creep into his own room.

'The window's shut!' hissed Anna, who could see much better than Tony in the dark.

'Oh no!' Tony was taken aback. It was true. As they came nearer, he could see that the windows were indeed fastened from the inside. Not even the little one at the top was open.

'Now I'll have to ring the bell,' he said worriedly, 'and they'll find out everything.'

'Say you went for a walk,' suggested Anna.

'I'll tell them the truth,' said Tony. 'They'll never believe it anyway.'

Anna went with him to the front door. Tony took off the cloak and gave it to her. She was suddenly looking rather sad.

'Bye, Tony,' she said softly, and without a backward glance, she vanished into the night.

CHAPTER FOURTEEN
Some Awkward Questions

As Tony went up in the lift, he tried to imagine what his parents would say. Would they be worried? Or furious? Or what? When he stepped out of the lift and saw that the door of the flat was shut, he knew he was in for it. Normally, when he rang the answerphone downstairs, there was someone standing at the open doorway to welcome him.

He pushed the doorbell and waited. He heard his mother's footsteps approaching, and the door opened.

'Do you know how late it is?' was her greeting.

'Nine o'clock?' Tony hazarded hopefully.

'It's a quarter to ten!' said his mother angrily. 'We've been waiting for you since eight o'clock. You've got some explaining to do, young man!' She marched him back to the living room, where his father was sitting on the sofa. When Tony came in, he stood up and turned off the television. Things were really looking bad!

'Where have you been?' asked his father.

'Me? Oh, just out for a walk.' Tony tried to sound innocent.

'I see. For a walk. At half past nine at night, my nine-year-old son takes it into his head to go for a walk.' He paused, then added sarcastically, 'And may one inquire where His Lordship walked to?'

'Er, oh, round and about.'

'An illuminating piece of information!' The corners of his father's mouth had begun to twitch, which meant that he was getting very, very angry, and trying to conceal it.

'There's such a funny smell,' said his mother suddenly. 'Is it you, Tony?' Tony felt himself being scrutinised from head to toe, and involuntarily, he too glanced down, hoping that there was no tell-tale sign, like earth from the cemetery on his shoes, of where he had been. Luckily, he was in the clear.

'Have you been burning something?' asked his mother.

'No,' said Tony. Here comes the Inquisition, he thought to himself.

'Perhaps somebody else made a fire, and you were "just looking"?'

'No.'

'Have you been smoking?'

'No.'

'Why do you smell of smoke, then?'

'Dunno. Perhaps it was Anna.'

'Anna?' His parents' ears pricked up. 'Who is Anna?'

'A girlfriend.'

'A *what*?'

'She's Rudolph's sister.'

'*Whose* sister?' shouted his father. 'Did you say Rudolph's?'

'Yes,' said Tony, who could not understand why his father was so upset.

107

'Are you sure you are telling the truth?' asked his father.

'Yes,' protested Tony.

'OK. We'll prove it.'

'Are you going to ring up?' asked Tony's mother.

Dad nodded, and opened the telephone directory. 'Ah, here we are. Appleby, Henry.'

'Who is Henry Appleby?' asked Tony warily. His father threw him a scornful look.

'Well, well. Imagine you not knowing who Appleby is,' he said, dialling the number. Someone at the other end of the line must have answered almost immediately, for he went on in quite a different voice: 'Mr Appleby? It's Peasbody here. I'm sorry to disturb you, there's just a little matter I'd like to clear up. My son here claims that your daughter Anna . . . What? Haven't . . . ?' He paused. 'I see. Thank you very much. Good night.'

He put down the receiver and turned to Tony. 'Did you know that your friend Rudolph doesn't have a sister? He's only got a brother, and his name is Leo.'

'Leo?' asked Tony.

'And as for the so-called Rudolph – he's not called Rudolph at all, nor even Rudolph Nigel, but just plain simple Nigel.'

'Nigel?' Tony was nonplussed. Then suddenly light dawned: they must be talking about the Nigel he had managed to smuggle in to tea in Rudolph's place. A terrible thought occurred to him: after all,

Nigel's nickname was Blabber-Mouth. Perhaps he had rung Tony's parents and blown it all? He could hardly believe that Nigel would be such a traitor.

'Well?' asked his father. 'What have you got to say?'

'I've always known him as Rudolph,' said Tony woodenly.

'And his sister?'

'She's called Anna, like I said.'

'Damn you, boy! Haven't I just told you Nigel hasn't got a sister?'

'Rudolph has,' said Tony stubbornly.

At this point, his mother decided to try the reasoning approach. 'Tony,' she said, 'you must realise that it seems very strange to us. You say you have been out for a walk with a girl who simply doesn't exist. Can't you tell us the truth?'

'I don't know what to say any more,' sighed Tony.

'All right, then,' said his father, who was having to make a visible effort to control himself. 'I recognised your so-called "Rudolph". He's the son of a colleague of mine at work, and he's called Nigel Appleby, not Rudolph Sackville-Bagg.'

'Why didn't you say earlier?' asked Tony.

His father gasped for air. 'Because I wanted to hear what you had to say about it.'

At least Tony now knew what the position was.

'I think that we still haven't met the real Rudolph,' put in Tony's mother slowly. 'I believe there really is someone called Rudolph, with a sister called Anna. But why haven't you let us meet him?'

Tony had to smile. His mother's cool, thoughtful approach had brought her a lot closer to the truth than all his father's rantings and ravings.

'You see,' he explained, 'you kept going on at me to bring Rudolph home. But Rudolph didn't want to come, so I asked Nigel instead. By the way,' he added as an afterthought, 'I really didn't know that Nigel's surname was Appleby.'

'Why didn't Rudolph want to come?' asked his mother.

'Because he always stays up so late, so he's sleepy, and also he doesn't like cake. He's a bit funny.'

His mother laughed. 'That doesn't matter. I enjoy meeting strange people. And if he doesn't want to eat anything, he needn't.'

'He'd be embarrassed,' said Tony. 'And also, he stinks.'

At this, even his father laughed. 'You certainly do pick your friends!' he said.

'He doesn't really know how to behave,' continued Tony.

'That doesn't matter either,' remarked his mother. 'What really counts in a person is their heart, and I'm sure your Rudolph has a good heart, Tony.'

Tony blanched. 'A good heart? What do you mean?' he said. Had Mum guessed what Rudolph was like?

But her face was all smiles. 'I mean, he's someone you can rely on,' she explained. 'Someone who won't leave you in the lurch.'

'Oh, er, yes,' Tony was very relieved.

'If you like him,' continued his mother, 'I think we would like him too.'

'Do you think so?' Tony sounded doubtful. 'Do you like vampires, then?'

'You're not starting that vampire craze again, are you?' laughed his father.

His mother looked cross. 'I don't think it's very funny,' she said.

Dad laughed even more loudly. 'So when do we get to meet this famous vampire of yours?' he asked.

'Um – I'll have to ask him,' said Tony. 'Next week, perhaps?' He suddenly felt exhausted, and longed to be able to creep into bed.

'I should keep your window shut,' called his mother as he reached the door. 'There have been the most enormous moths flying around in the last few weeks.'

'OK,' said Tony, turning round quickly so parents would not see his smile. 'Good night.'

CHAPTER FIFTEEN
Prying Parents

'You haven't been very wide awake today, have you?' remarked Tony's father the following evening. They were sitting on the sofa waiting for the beginning of a wildlife documentary on television.

Tony yawned. 'I think I'll go to bed,' he said.

'Your "walk" yesterday must have tired you out!' teased his father.

'Actually, it was the maths homework,' corrected Tony. Whoever said schooldays were the happiest of your life?

'Could you do it all?' asked his mother.

'Of course,' replied Tony.

At that moment, the telephone rang. Tony's father picked up the receiver. 'Peasbody here,' he said in his special telephone voice. Then a puzzled look came over his face. 'Who did you want to speak to? Are you sure you've got the right number? Hold on a moment.' He covered the receiver with his hand. 'It's some crazy girl,' he whispered. 'I can hardly understand what she is saying. She hisses. Is it some kid at your school?'

'Can't be,' said Tony's mother, hurriedly taking the receiver from him. 'Mrs Peasbody here. Who's speaking, please? Who? You want to talk to Tony?' Her forehead wrinkled in disbelief. 'It's for you,' she whispered.

'Who is it?' asked Tony's father.

Mum shrugged her shoulders. 'I've no idea. She spoke as if she had her hand over her mouth.'

By this time. Tony had the receiver in his hand. 'Hello?' he said. A soft giggle came from the other end. 'Who is it?' he asked.

'Anna!' came the answer, soft and squeaky, but quite clearly.

Tony went pale. 'Y-you?' he stammered. This was a fine kettle of fish! To make matters worse, he had a parent on either side of him, listening to every word.

'Who is it?' demanded his father.

'Anna.' It was an unwilling reply.

'What does she want?' hissed his mother.

'I don't know,' said Tony through clenched teeth. 'I haven't had a chance to find out!'

'Are you still mad at me?' Anna was asking. 'About yesterday? Because I know I...'

'No, no, of course not,' Tony reassured her hurriedly.

'I've got a surprise for you!' she said.

'A surprise?' Out of the comer of his eye, he saw his parents exchange a meaningful look. 'What sort of surprise?' he asked.

'A story!' she said. 'A real vampire love story,' At these last words, she was so overcome with giggles that Tony could hardly hear her. 'Can I come round and read it to you this evening?'

'Er, no, not this evening. Tomorrow perhaps.'

'OK. Tomorrow. What time?'

Tony glanced at his parents and thought for a moment. 'My grandmother has nine clocks,' he said, and was pleased to see the look of complete bewilderment which passed between them. Serve them right for eavesdropping!

Luckily Anna had understood. 'At nine o'clock. OK.'

'What's Rudolph doing?'

'He's already gone,' explained Anna. 'He was starving.'

'Oh, I see.' As always, when the vampires' eating habits were mentioned, Tony felt rather sick. 'Well, say hi to him from me,' he said, at a loss for words. Why did his parents have to stand so close to him? Why couldn't they go into the kitchen for a while?

'Bye, then,' he said.

'See you tomorrow,' said Anna, and hung up.

'What's this? Finished already?' said Dad in mock astonishment.

'Yes,' growled Tony.

'What was that you said about Gran having nine clocks?' asked his mother.

'Oh, just a joke.'

'Why didn't you invite Anna round when Rudolph comes?' his father wanted to know.

'I didn't think of it.'

'What about Rudolph?' asked his mother. 'Have you fixed a day yet?'

'No. I haven't seen him.'

'Doesn't he go to school?'

Tony had to laugh. 'No,' he said.

'Oh?' His mother was very surprised.

'He has a...tutor,' said Tony. He had read somewhere that you could have a tutor instead of going to school.

'Good gracious! Is he ill?' asked his mother.

'No, not exactly. But he sleeps too late to go to school.'

His mother shook her head incredulously. 'What you kids get away with!' she said.

'I agree,' said Dad with a smile. 'Quite astonishing.'

'I'm glad you think so!' said Tony crossly, and went out, slamming the door behind him. First they eavesdropped, then they interrogated him, and now they laughed at him! No wonder he was cross!

CHAPTER SIXTEEN
Rendezvous in Pyjamas

The following evening, Tony was ready for bed unusually early. He had already had a wash and was in his pyjamas at half past seven.

'You're not going to bed already, are you?' His mother was astonished.

'I want to read,' explained Tony.

'All right. But lights out at eight, remember?'

'OK. Goodnight.'

Once in his room. Tony half-closed the curtains. It was still so light that he did not need to turn on the lamp. He took down his new book, *Tales of the Otherworld*, from his shelf, climbed into bed and began to read. The first story suited his mood exactly: it was about two boys who went to a lonely inn one night and...

Soft footsteps crossed the hall, and Tony jerked upright in fright. Then he remembered it was only his mother coming to see if he was still reading, and he quickly hid the book under his pillow and pretended to be asleep. The door opened quietly and closed again almost immediately. The footsteps went back across the hall. That meant he could relax and forget about his parents, because they thought he was asleep. He settled himself comfortably once more, and switched on the light, then pulled out his book and searched for the right page.

A sudden tapping on the window made him jump. Outside, it was almost dark, so he could only see a faint shadow. He put down the book and went to the window. There on the sill sat Anna. Tony pushed the curtain to one side and opened the window.

'Hi, Tony,' said Anna, slipping into the room as noiselessly as a cat.

'Hello,' replied Tony, feeling himself blush. It was just as well it was dark!

'Do I smell nice?' she asked happily, beaming at him.

'Oh, er, yes,' murmured Tony. What else could he say? She would not be pleased if he said she smelt of a mixture of dead leaves, moth balls and mildew!

'It's my special perfume,' she explained. 'It's called "Fragrant Earth".'

'I've never heard of that before,' said Tony.

'That's not surprising,' Anna said proudly. 'My mother makes it herself. It's only for vampires.' With these words, she came up close to Tony and bared her neck. 'Can you smell it? Isn't it devilishly delicious?'

'Mmm,' said Tony evasively. He had seldom smelt anything quite so revolting in his life. 'It's ... er, very powerful.'

'Isn't it,' she agreed. 'We are only allowed to wear it on very special occasions.'

'It reminds me of onions,' went on Tony, whose eyes were beginning to water.

'Its main ingredient is onions,' said Anna. 'Then you mix in a bit of deadly nightshade, and some cow dung.'

'Ugh!' Tony could not stop himself.

Anna looked hurt. 'I thought you liked it,' she said.

'Oh, yes, I do,' said Tony quickly. 'It's just a bit unusual.'

'Shall we put on some music?' suggested Anna, changing the subject.

Tony looked nervously at the door. 'Better not,' he said. 'Mum and Dad think I'm asleep.'

'Oh.' She sounded disappointed. Then she brightened. 'Never mind. I've brought you something to read. A real vampire love story,' She reached under her cloak and drew out a bundle of yellowing pages, which she smoothed flat carefully. Tony noticed they were covered with a round, childish handwriting.

'Did you write it?' he asked.

Anna looked embarrassed. 'Yes,' she admitted, and began to read: 'Once upon a time there was a King and Queen, who longed to have a child – but in vain. However, one day the Queen was bathing in a pool, and it so happened that a frog hopped out of the water onto the bank and said: "Your wish will come true." And sure enough, before a year had passed, the Queen gave birth to a baby boy. The joyful parents decided to have a feast to celebrate. As well as all their friends and relations, they invited the fairies to bring their son luck. However, there were thirteen fairies in the kingdom, and the Queen only had twelve golden plates, so one fairy did not receive an invitation. The feast was the most magnificent anyone could remember, and at the end, each fairy gave the child a gift: one blessed him with health, one with intelligence, another with good looks, and so on, until eleven had given him their blessing. At that moment, the thirteenth fairy, the one who had not been invited, burst into the hall and cackled: "This is my gift! When he is fifteen, your son will prick his finger on a spindle and fall down dead!" Luckily, the twelfth fairy had not yet given her gift, and although she could not take away the spell completely, she was able to lessen its effect. "He will not die," she said, "but will fall into a deep sleep which will last for a hundred years."'

'Oh yes?' said Tony. 'A hundred years?' The story was becoming familiar!

'The King decided to protect his son from this fate, and so he gave the order that every spindle in the kingdom should be burned. It so happened that, on the prince's fifteenth birthday the King and Queen were away from the palace. The boy decided to explore, and found himself at last at the foot of an old turret. He climbed the narrow staircase and reached a tiny door at the top. In the lock was a rusty key, and as he turned it, the door sprang open and there, in a little room, sat an old woman spinning flax. "What is that, bobbing up and down?" asked the prince. He took the spindle to see for himself, and at once the magic spell was fulfilled: he pricked his finger and fell on the nearby bed in a deep sleep. At that moment, everyone else in the palace was overcome by the same sleep. The King and Queen had just arrived home, and they fell asleep. The entire court fell asleep. Even the horses in the stable, the dogs in the yard, the pigeons on the rooftop and the flies on the walls, everything slept.

'A hedge of thorns grew up around the castle, growing higher every year so that eventually nothing could be seen of the palace behind it. Tales of the handsome young prince were spread abroad in the land, and from time to time, princesses came to try to break through the hedge. They were never successful, however, for the thorn branches were twisted together like linked hands, and the princesses became caught fast and died a terrible death. At last, after many years, a certain princess happened to come to that part of the country. An old man told her the story of the castle behind the wall of thorns, and the princess declared: "I'm not afraid! I shall try to reach this handsome prince!" What the old man did not realise was that this particular princess was in fact a vampire. She turned herself into a bat and flew over the hedge. Once in the courtyard of the castle, she saw the dogs and horses lying fast asleep, and venturing further inside, she found the entire court sleeping as well. Finally she came to the tower with the little room where the King's son lay. He was so handsome that she could not take her eyes off him, and she bent down and gave him a vampire kiss. He stirred and opened his eyes and looked at her happily. It did not take long before he was a vampire too, and the pair of them lived happily ever after.'

'I know that story,' said Tony. 'It's the same as *Sleeping Beauty*.'

'My version's better though!' laughed Anna.

'You forgot the court,' reproached Tony, 'and the King and Queen. Did they turn into vampires as well?'

'I haven't decided yet,' said Anna. 'I wanted to ask you about it. You don't think that would make it too grisly?'

'Why should it?' asked Tony. 'After all, no one believes these tales of vampires nowadays...'

'What?' said Anna furiously. 'No one believes in vampires? What about you? Don't you believe in us?'

'Oh, er, yes, I do, of course,' Tony reassured her hurriedly. 'But everyone else...'

'Everyone else? I thought everyone was frightened of us.'

''Fraid not.' Tony shook his head. 'Last week, for instance, we had to write a composition. The title was "A Terrifying Experience". I went up to our teacher and asked her whether we were allowed to write about vampires, and she just laughed. "Vampires?" she said, loud enough for the whole class to hear. "Vampires belong to fairy tales, Tony.

No, now you are in Year Four, you must write about something that really happened.'"

'What an old goat!' snorted Anna. 'What did you write about in the end?'

'Something I saw on the television once.'

'Did she notice?'

'No, she thought it was quite lively and realistic, and gave me five out of ten.'

'Huh!' said Anna. 'You'd have got ten out of ten for a vampire story! What about your parents? Don't they believe in us?'

Tony shook his head. 'They least of all. But they would like to meet you. You have been invited to tea.'

'Really?' Anna's face lit up. 'At last I'll be able to meet your parents, Tony!' She clapped her hands and gave a little jump. 'Are they as nice as you?'

'Er, I suppose so,' Tony was embarrassed.

'When can we come?'

'Next Wednesday?' suggested Tony. It was the first day that came into his head. 'Do you think Rudolph will come too?'

'I'll ask him at once!' she said, and jumped up onto the windowsill. 'Bye, then – see you on Wednesday!'

'W-wait a minute!' stuttered Tony. 'Are you really going to come?'

'You bet!' she smiled, and vanished.

CHAPTER SEVENTEEN
Final Preparations

'Come on, Tony,' said his mother the following Wednesday. 'Help me whip this cream.'

'It's much too early still,' protested Tony.

'Nonsense!' declared his mother. 'It's almost five o'clock.'

'That makes no difference. They always have an afternoon rest.'

His mother gave him a searching look. 'I'm sure even you don't really believe that.'

'Yes, I promise, it's true. It's good for their health.' What a business it all was! He did not think vampires ever got up before sunset, and that would mean they might not arrive until eight o'clock! And Mum was already putting the kettle on and heating the milk for the cocoa!

'Er, Mum,' began Tony. 'I think I ought to explain – er, they might not come until eight o'clock.'

'Come on now, Tony,' said his mother. 'It's almost your bedtime at eight.'

'I know,' replied Tony.

'Well – don't Rudolph and Anna have to go to bed as well?'

'No,' said Tony, trying not to laugh.

'Funny way to bring up kids!' grumbled his mother. 'What's going to happen to all the tea?' She waved a hand vaguely in the direction of the kettle and the pan of milk. 'Everything's nearly ready!'

'We could have our tea now, and then have some apple juice later on,' suggested Tony.

His mother poured some water into the teapot. 'What about getting off to school tomorrow morning?'

'Oh, come on, Mum, just this once!' pleaded Tony.

His mother stirred the cocoa powder crossly into the milk. 'Well, all right,' she conceded. 'But I'm not at all pleased, and I'm only saying yes because I'm dying to meet these strange friends of yours.'

Tony gave a quiet sigh of relief.

'What about all these cakes?' she went on.

'I'll eat them,' offered Tony. His mother had bought cream buns again, and this time there were eight of them! At least it would make up for the last time when Nigel had scoffed the lot, and he hadn't had any.

'You may have two,' said his mother. 'Then we'll have the rest later this evening.'

'Great!' Tony could hardly believe his luck. Not only had his mother agreed to let him stay up late, but now he was getting two extra buns as well!

'Here, you can have some cocoa too,' said his mother, handing him a steaming mugful.

'Mmm, thanks.' Tony took the mug and the buns and went off to his room. He had already finished his homework, so he could read in peace – and in just about three hours, the party would begin!

CHAPTER EIGHTEEN
A Lively Evening

Shortly after eight, the front doorbell rang. Tony had been looking at the clock every few minutes for the past half hour, and now a shiver of expectancy ran through him. He hoped all would go well, and that Rudolph really had come as well. What would his parents say? Tony was so excited that his legs nearly would not carry him out of his room.

His parents had already opened the door. 'Good evening,' he heard Rudolph say in his grating voice, followed almost immediately by Anna's piping: 'Hello!'

'Good evening!' replied his mother, taking a couple of steps backwards. 'Come in!'

'So here you are at last!' Dad was doing his best to sound welcoming, but even his blustery voice sounded rather taken aback.

He had good reason: Rudolph and Anna looked quite a sight. They had put rouge on their cheeks and smeared red lipstick on their lips. Their faces, which were normally chalk-white, were caked with brownish powder, but it had been put on in patches, so that there were still places where white gleamed through. The penetrating smell of 'Fragrant Earth' hung pungently about the pair of them.

'This is for you,' said Rudolph holding out a bunch of greenery to Tony's mother.

'Thank you,' she murmured, fingering the stems gingerly. They had clearly been torn from a hedge somewhere.

'Aren't they pretty?' said Anna. 'There are plenty like that growing at home.'

'Ssh!' Rudolph hissed at her furiously. It was clear even to Tony that the sprigs were from the box hedge which grew in the cemetery.

'I'll go and put them in water,' said his mother, disappearing into the kitchen.

'Where is Tony, I wonder?' said Dad.

'Here,' replied Tony, who had been watching their meeting from a distance.

'Tony!' said Anna, her face reddening. 'How are you?'

'Oh, I'm fine,' said Tony, and he blushed an equally deep crimson.

'Hello, Tony,' said Rudolph, shaking him by the hand. Rudolph's hand felt cold and knobbly, like the hand of a skeleton. It was the first time that Tony had ever touched Rudolph's hand, and it made him shiver. Perhaps it was because they both looked so strange and unfamiliar tonight. They must have come straight from the vault, in which case they could not have had anything to eat. In fact, Rudolph was looking quite drained and weak.

'Er, are you hungry?' Tony asked cautiously.

'Yes.' said Rudolph. 'Very.'

'Come on in, then,' said Tony's father, trying to sound jovial. 'Everything's ready. There are some buns and fruit juice.' He led the way into the living room.

'Is there milk as well?' whispered Anna. Tony nodded.

His parents had laid the table with the best china, and decorated it with paper napkins and candles – everything looked lovely...except the two visitors! The same thought obviously occurred to Anna, who looked rather embarrassed and wandered uncertainly round the table. 'How pretty it looks!' she said. 'We never have anything like this at home.'

'Ssh!' frowned Rudolph.

'Why shouldn't I say that?' argued Anna. She turned to Tony's father and said: 'It's true. We always eat out.'

'Do you?' said Tony's mother conversationally, returning with the box sprigs in a vase. 'It must get very expensive to eat out all the time.'

'Actually, it's quite cheap!' Rudolph could not help smiling, and for a moment his pointed teeth were revealed. He quickly covered his mouth with his hand.

'That box does smell odd!' remarked Tony's father. 'Shall I open a window?'

'No – I'd rather you didn't,' said Mum. 'Otherwise those moths will get in.'

'Moths?' giggled Rudolph. 'I love moths!'

'Well, I don't,' said Tony's mother firmly.

'Bats are even better. They have such sweet faces!'

'Ugh!' shivered Tony's mother.

'Or vampires!' Anna could not resist the suggestion, and this time it was too much for Rudolph. He broke into a peal of laughter, but as he still had his hand over his mouth, he soon ran out of air and began to choke.

'Are you all right?' asked Mum, but Rudolph could only cough.

'Wait a minute!' said Tony's mother, and ran to the kitchen, returning with a glass of water. 'Drink this – you'll feel much better.'

By this time, Rudolph was coughing so badly that he did not notice that Tony's mother was holding a glass to his lips. But he had barely tasted the first drop before he sprang up, and ran into the hallway, sneezing and spluttering.

'You poor thing!' said Tony's mother, hurrying after him.

Anna looked at Tony and grinned. 'What can you expect?' she said. 'Water on an empty stomach...'

At this point, Tony's mother came back. 'He's locked himself in the bathroom,' she said, 'and there are the most terrible noises coming from inside!'

To soothe her, Anna said calmly: 'It's only because he's so hungry.'

This did not seem a very adequate explanation to Tony's mother, but his father asked: 'Haven't either of you had anything to eat, then?'

Anna shook her head.

'Well, come on, come on!' He held out the plate of cream buns, and Anna took one.

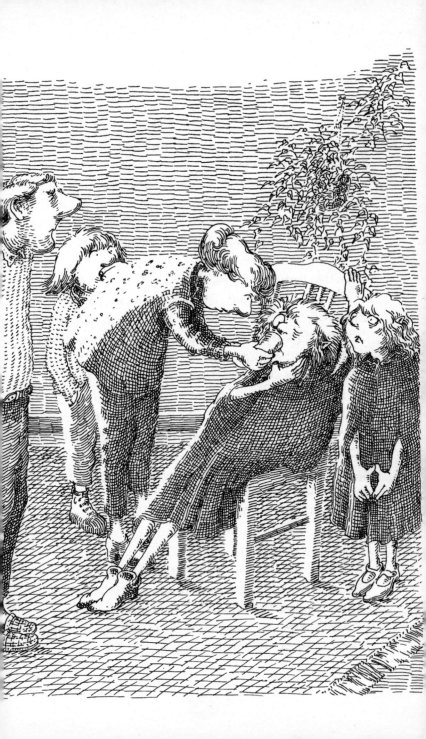

'Go on, then,' urged Tony's father. 'No need to wait!'

'I – er – don't like cake,' she said.

'Oh. Well, just eat the cream, then,' said Tony's father. Anna looked pleased, and began to lick the cream off the bun.

'Would you like some apple juice?' asked Tony's mother.

'No thank you. It gives me a tummy ache.'

'What do you like to drink, then?'

'Milk, if you have any.'

'Of course,' said Tony's mother. 'I'll fetch some.' As she went into the hall, she let out a cry. 'Rudolph's disappeared!' she exclaimed, and Tony heard her hurrying around anxiously, opening all the doors. 'How could he have got out of the flat?'

'Through the front door?' suggested Dad helpfully.

'No!' wailed Mum. 'We would have noticed him!'

'Perhaps we just weren't looking at the right moment?'

'Don't be silly!' insisted Mum. 'He would have had to have gone right past the living-room door.'

'Well, he must have flown, then,' said Dad crossly.

'Who knows?' said Mum. 'Tony's bedroom window is open.'

'What?' exclaimed Tony. *He* had not opened it! But of course, he must not let the others know that.

'Oh, yes, I left it open,' he added hurriedly.

'There you are! A perfectly reasonable explanation!' said his father.

If only he knew. Mum had nearly hit the nail on the head, as usual!

'I suppose I just haven't looked in the right place!' said Mum in a small voice, sitting down once more.

Dad turned to Anna. 'Your brother can't fly, can he?' he asked.

'Of course not!' said Anna.

'I knew it! You see, Hilary? The things you dream up!'

Tony's mother looked at Anna warily. Tony wondered if she was suspicious; his father would never notice a thing, but Mum was different...

'May I have my milk?' asked Anna.

'Oh, of course. I'd forgotten,' said Tony's mother. 'Tony, be a dear and fetch it!' Grudgingly, Tony got to his feet.

'Milk is very good for you,' said Anna. 'It makes you strong.'

Tony returned with the milk, and put the glass down in front of her. 'Thank you!' she smiled, and emptied the glass in one gulp. For a moment, nobody said anything. Then Dad remarked, 'So you have a fancy dress costume, too?'

'Yes,' nodded Anna, not at all abashed.

'Where do you hold all these Hallowe'en parties?'

'In private,' said Anna, looking smug. Tony looked at her admiringly. He would never have thought of such a good answer on the spur of the moment like that.

'I wonder what you look like in something other than a costume,' said Tony's father.

Tony's heart nearly stopped beating, but Anna simply shrugged her shoulders casually and said: 'Oh, not much different. Perhaps a bit prettier!'

'Prettier?' Tony's father laughed hollowly. 'You're certainly not vain, anyway!'

'No,' agreed Anna.

'Or shy.'

Anna looked at Tony. 'Sometimes I am,' she said.

'So you and your brother always go to these parties together?'

'Yes. We do nearly everything together.'

'Don't you ever quarrel?'

'Of course. He has a very old-fashioned outlook on certain things.'

'Really? Such as?'

'Oh – anything to do with girls. *He* thinks boys are tougher than girls.'

'Aren't they?' asked Dad.

'Don't tell me you agree with him?' said Anna crossly, her face turning quite red.

'No, no,' soothed Tony's father, 'but you must admit most girls would rather wear pretty dresses than go off climbing trees and getting themselves in a mess.'

'No, you've got it all wrong!' said Anna fiercely. 'Why do girls wear pretty dresses? Only because their mothers like to dress them up. And then they don't climb trees because they are not supposed to get their clothes dirty.'

'Exactly,' agreed Tony's mother.

'But what about boys?' went on Tony's father. 'Boys play with cars, and girls play with dolls.'

Anna looked exasperated. 'You just don't understand,' she said.

'What do you think, Tony?' asked his father.

Tony hesitated. 'I think girls are stupid,' he said finally. 'They're always giggling, and they get knocked over even when they're just playing netball!'

'Well, I think boys are silly too. They never let girls play football with them!' declared Anna.

'Is your brother like that?' asked Tony's mother.

Anna nodded. 'Even though the first of our line was a lady.'

'What did you say? The first in your line? Are you just stringing us along?' joked Dad.

Tony went hot and cold all over. Now Anna really had gone too far! But no, she was not so easily disturbed. 'I meant our first ancestor,' she explained. 'She was called Cleo Hermione Victoria Charlotte Sabina Sackville-Bagg, the vampire.'

'That's a very splendid-sounding name,' said Tony's father.

'It's too long,' said Anna, 'so it's been shortened.'

'You sound a funny lot in your family,' said Tony's father, laughing.

'Do you think so?' Anna looked put out. 'Most people who have anything to do with us don't think we are the least bit funny.'

'Really?' probed Dad. 'What do they think of you, then?'

'I would prefer not to tell you,' said Anna with dignity. 'And now, I must be going.' She stood up and smoothed her cloak.

'You'll come again soon, won't you?' asked Dad. 'Tony will be so sad if you don't,' he added mischievously.

'Really?' asked Anna, looking tenderly at Tony. 'Well, in that case...' She began to blush, and quickly went out into the hall.

'Wait a minute!' called Dad. 'You're going the wrong way. The front door's on the left!'

'Oh, of course.' Anna sounded rather surprised. Out of habit, she had automatically turned in the direction of Tony's bedroom and the open window. Pulling herself together, she marched out of the front door, said goodbye, and even went down to the ground floor in the lift.

EPILOGUE

'What a nice girl!' said Tony's father when they were all once more round the table. 'Did you like her, Hilary?'

'I thought she was rather odd.'

'Odd? Why?'

'Her pale little face – the funny cloak – her voice – I don't know.'

'What about Rudolph, then?'

'He was even worse! Those bloodshot eyes and bony fingers!'

'But they're only children!' laughed Dad. 'You sound as if you were frightened out of your wits, my dear!'

'What wits?' giggled Tony.

His father looked at him sharply. 'We don't want any of your cheek!' he said sternly. 'It was you who brought up all this vampire nonsense.'

'I did not!' retorted Tony. 'Vampires have been around since the Middle Ages!'

'Oh yes? How do you know?'

'I read it in a book.'

'In one of your horror stories, I suppose.'

'No, actually, in a dictionary.'

'Really?' asked Tony's mother, sounding genuinely interested. 'I'd like to see that myself – in ours?'

'No,' answered Tony. 'In the one at school.'

'Well, it might be in ours as well,' said his mother hopefully, going over to the bookcase. She took out a book, leafed through it, and read: 'Vampires: according to myth, these are bodies of the dead, who leave their coffins at night to suck the blood of humans.'

'Yes, yes, we know all that. There are other things according to myth, like...'

'...witches, dwarfs, ghosts and fairies!' chanted Tony, who remembered only too well the first conversation he had had with his parents on the subject of vampires.

'So you see, there's nothing to worry about,' reassured Dad, 'unless you're going to believe in dwarfs and fairies as well.'

'Of course I'm not!' said Mum crossly.

'And probably Rudolph and Anna will try to look a little more normal when they come next time, won't they, Tony?'

'Mmm,' said Tony doubtfully.

'Well, as far as I'm concerned, I'd be glad if it was a while before they came again,' said Mum.

'I'm sure Tony won't agree!' laughed Dad.

'I don't!' said Tony starkly. He had almost choked on his cream bun. 'I suppose now you're going to forbid me ever to play with Rudolph and Anna again?'

'No, no, we wouldn't go as far as that,' said his mother, 'but surely we can have our own opinion about your friends, can't we?'

'Suppose so,' Tony reluctantly had to agree.

'I think they are creepy,' said Mum, 'and if there really were such things as vampires, I'm sure they would look just like your two friends!'

Dad laughed, as though Mum had made a good joke. 'But there aren't such things as vampires,' he said. 'The pair of them are nothing more sinister than two normal kids who have delved a bit too deeply into their grandmother's dressing-up box.' He took a cream bun and munched on it, and for a while nobody said anything.

Then Tony grumbled, 'Well, it was you who kept going on about meeting them, anyway. I did warn you about them.'

'Yes, I must admit, you did,' smiled his mother. 'Oh well, I suppose I'll get used to them eventually.'

'And you won't go on any more about this vampire nonsense, will you, Tony?' said Dad.

Tony gave a rueful grin. 'OK,' he said. Poor old Dad still did not have a clue, and Mum's suspicions would soon quieten down. All had turned out well in the end.

'I'm off to bed,' he said. 'Goodnight.'

'Goodnight, dear,' replied his parents.

It was with a feeling of great contentment and satisfaction that Tony finally climbed into bed and pulled the covers up over his head.

THE GHOST PRISON

JOSEPH DELANEY

Illustrated by Scott M. Fischer

'This is the entrance to the Witch Well and behind that door you'd face your worst nightmare. Don't ever go through there.'

Night falls, the portcullis rises in the moonlight, and young Billy starts his first night as a prison guard. But this is no ordinary prison. There are haunted cells that can't be used, whispers and cries in the night . . . and the dreaded Witch Well. Billy is warned to stay away from the prisoner down in the Witch Well. But who could it be? What prisoner could be so frightening? Billy is about to find out . . .

'Will satisfy the most hardened fan of horror'
The Times

'Spine-tingling'
LoveReading

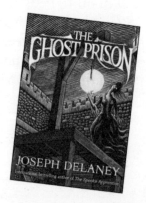

9781783443208